# Homeless in New York

Alex Telman

Published by Alex Telman, 2024.

HOMELESS IN NEW YORK

**First edition. November 17, 2024.**

Copyright © 2024 Alex Telman.

ISBN: 979-8230372066

Written by Alex Telman.

# Table of Contents

# Author's Note

Dear Reader,

Homeless in New York was born from the streets themselves, from the raw, unvarnished reality that pulses beneath the glossy exterior of the city. New York, with its iconic skyline and endless energy, is a place where dreams are both made and shattered. Yet for many, the city's dreams are nothing more than a mirage—distant, elusive, and ultimately out of reach. This collection is a journey through the city's underbelly, where survival is a daily fight, and humanity is often overlooked in favor of progress.

As a writer, I've always been drawn to the untold stories—the voices that society ignores, the lives discarded and forgotten in the cracks between the glimmering towers. The homeless in New York, to me, are the true witnesses of the city's contradictions. They live on the margins, but in their struggle, they hold a kind of wisdom, a raw truth that most people are too uncomfortable to confront. These poems are their stories—stories of resilience, loss, survival, and yes, even hope.

In writing these poems, I wanted to capture not just the physicality of life on the streets, but the emotional and psychological toll that comes with it. I wanted to give voice to the invisible, to show the humanity that's so often buried beneath the layers of poverty and shame. This collection is an invitation to step into their world, to see New York through their eyes, and to never forget that the homeless are not just statistics—they are people, with stories that matter.

— *Alex*

# Introduction

This book is a journey into the raw, unflinching heart of New York City—the side you're not supposed to see. It's a world where the streets, slick with rain, pulse with the life of the forgotten. Where dreams are torn between the glitz of Times Square and the shadows under the bridges. These poems are not for the faint of heart. They are for those willing to look directly into the eyes of despair and hope in equal measure. *Homeless in New York* is a collection that refuses to let the invisibility of the homeless remain intact. It takes what is often ignored or romanticized—the empty bottles, the cracked sidewalks, the sleepless nights—and pulls them into sharp, painful focus.

In the first poem, *The Streets of Manhattan*, we dive headfirst into the gritty landscape where survival is a daily battle. Here, the street isn't a road, it's a weapon—a battlefield where only the strong or the lucky survive. *Fifth Avenue, Empty Pocket* contrasts the dazzling wealth of one of the most famous streets in the world with the desperate, gnawing emptiness of a life without money, without a place to call home. The city might be a playground for the rich, but to the homeless, it's an unyielding jungle that feeds on your misery.

*Sleeping Under the Bridge* captures the cold truth of what it's like to be forgotten, to sleep in places that aren't meant for rest, to face the suffocating weight of invisibility. In *Skid Row Dreams*, the people on the edges of society dream, but their dreams are the cracked reflections of a life they can barely remember. In *I Have a Dream*, the poem twists the notion of the American dream, revealing how the homeless, in their fractured sleep, long for the most basic human need—security. Yet each morning, they wake to the nightmare of survival.

These are not just poems—they are a call to awareness, a demand for recognition. They explore the divide between the warmth of the coffee shop window in *Coffee Shop Window* and the icy exclusion of the homeless soul staring in, separated by glass and a social barrier too thick to break. The city that never sleeps hums with activity, yet in *The City That Never Sleeps, and Neither Do I*, it becomes clear that the restless minds of those without homes beat in time with the pulse of New York, caught between the energy of the city and the weariness of the body that won't stop.

Through the isolation and the hardships, the people of this book find moments of beauty and connection, however fleeting. In *The Train Car Symphony*, the rumble of the subway, the touch of a stranger's glance, the warmth of a shared moment amid the chaos, all become part of the symphony of survival. But it's not all beauty; it's also about the brutality—the stench of the subway grate, the endless hunger, the brutal cold that gnaws at the bones and the pride.

Each poem offers a glimpse of what it means to live in a city that is both a beacon of opportunity and a machine that chews up the weak. But in all its darkness, there is also light—faint, flickering, and often out of reach, but it's there. From *The Forgotten Faces of Harlem* to *The Grit of the Lower East Side*, these poems show the resilience of those who refuse to be erased, who create communities under the shadows of the skyscrapers.

As you read through these poems, you will encounter the true face of homelessness in New York. It's not a single story but a thousand untold tales. The homeless have stories, too. Stories of dreams, stories of survival, stories of pain and resilience that refuse to be silenced.

*Homeless in New York* isn't just a collection of poems. It's a window into a world too often shut out, a harsh reality that demands your attention. It will make you uncomfortable. It will challenge you. But it will also make you see—see the people, the lives, the humanity that exists in every corner of this great city, no matter how far they are pushed to the margins. And maybe, just maybe, it will make you stop and ask: who are we when we stop seeing each other?

# The Streets of Manhattan

A gritty exploration of the landscape of survival in the city.

THEY SAID THE CITY would chew me up,

but they forgot to mention how it gnaws—

slow, steady, like a rat

dragging a piece of string through a hole in the wall,

hoping it'll lead to something better,

but the hole's already filled with shit.

I see them all,

the ones who hustle their way down Broadway,

tapping their shiny shoes to some dream that's already dying.

They look at the buildings

like they've got secrets,

but the buildings are empty inside—

full of glass and steel and nothing.

They're all just ghosts.

I've seen it—

people with their backs straight,

their collars stiff,

and the misery leaking out from under their skin,

like sweat on a summer sidewalk.

None of them know it yet,

but they're already dead.

I sleep in the park because the bench has

less spine than most of these people,

and at least it doesn't talk about how

my dreams are dirty.

I hear them complain,

but they don't know the half of it—

they've never known what it's like

to have nothing but your bones

and the sour taste of yesterday's whiskey

rolling around in your gut.

The subway comes,

it goes,

it's a tunnel of voices I can't hear.

The squeal of the train is a scream,

but nobody cares.

Not the banker with his head in his phone,

not the woman with the red lipstick

who pretends she's going somewhere.

I saw a rat today,

he had more guts than most of these suits.

He stole someone's half-eaten sandwich

and ate it right there,

his little paws holding onto it like

he had every right to.

And maybe he did.

I'm not asking for charity.

I don't need your pity.

But I could use a cigarette,

a dry pair of socks,

a clean corner to sit in for one goddamn minute

without someone telling me

that my broken shoes make me less human.

But that's the game, isn't it?

You don't get to play

unless you can pay.

And they don't want you here

unless you've got something

to sell or something to prove.

But I'm still here.

Not because I want to be,

# HOMELESS IN NEW YORK

but because there's nowhere else

for the ghosts to go.

I saw a man in a suit

step over a woman last night.

He didn't even look down.

Just kept walking,

his briefcase bouncing against his hip

like he had somewhere important to be.

I thought—

maybe he's running away from the truth too.

Maybe he thinks if he walks fast enough,

he can outrun the fact that he's no different than me—

just another rat in this maze,

pretending the walls don't close in.

Tomorrow I'll wake up,

stiff,

like the city that won't stop moving.

I'll drag my bones out of this cardboard cocoon

and watch the sky change color

as the sun burns through the lies.

And I'll wonder

if the city will finally swallow me whole

or if it's going to keep me hanging around

like some damn afterthought,

the way it does with everyone.

Either way,

I'll keep moving

because the city's always got somewhere for me to go—

it just doesn't care

whether I get there.

But that's the beauty of it,

isn't it?

We're all just shadows here—

moving,

striving,

but never quite real enough

to matter.

---

YOU EVER NOTICE HOW they act like they've got it all figured out? They walk around like kings and queens in their fancy suits, all stiff and shiny, thinking they're better than the rest of us. But here's the thing—none of them know they're already dead inside. You can see it in their eyes, in the way they look at the buildings, like they're looking for something. But those buildings are empty. Full of glass and steel and nothing. You think I'm the only one stuck in this city of ghosts? Hell no. They're all just stumbling around, pretending their shiny shoes can outrun the truth. But we're all just rats in this maze, trying to get out, pretending we're not trapped in the same filthy hole.

I sleep on a bench in the park, and at least it doesn't lie to me. It doesn't care about my dirty dreams or the whiskey on my breath. It doesn't tell me I'm less of a person because I've got no money, no job, no future. The bench is honest. The city isn't. The city doesn't care about anyone unless they're useful. And you know what? I'm not useful. I'm just here, waiting for something to change. But I've seen it. It won't change. The city's like a machine—it'll keep grinding, eating up everyone and spitting them out, whether you've got a fancy briefcase or nothing at all.

And that banker, the one who stepped over the woman? He doesn't even see her. Doesn't see me. Doesn't see anyone who isn't contributing to his precious little game. But that's what they all do, isn't it? They run, they run, pretending they're better than everyone else. Maybe they think if they walk fast enough, they can outrun the truth. But the truth is, they're no different than me. We're all just trying to survive this goddamn city, and we're all going to end up in the same hole. You can't outrun that.

But the city? It doesn't care if I make it or not. It'll keep moving, swallowing people whole, and I'll keep dragging my bones through it, because there's nowhere else for me to go. It's always got somewhere for me to be—but it doesn't give a damn whether I get there. That's the beauty of it, you know? The city doesn't care. We're all just shadows, moving, striving, but never real enough to matter.

# Fifth Avenue, Empty Pocket

The contrast between wealth and poverty on one of the world's most famous streets.

THEY MARCH IN THEIR thousand-dollar shoes,

their eyes gleaming with lies—

no soul, just polished leather

and something cold behind the glass.

Their teeth flash like knives

cutting through the city's veins,

ignoring the stench of rot in the gutters

where I sleep,

face down in the piss-soaked cracks

of their grand illusion.

I've got nothing left—

not a dime, not a prayer,

just this pile of rags

that once called itself a man.

The sun is too bright for this place—

I could burn under its gaze

if I had the strength to care.

They pass like ghosts in silk,

on their way to whatever it is

they're pretending is worth a damn.

They don't see me,

don't see the hole in the sky

where they keep their freedom,

as if a pocket full of green

could ever buy your soul.

A woman with a smile that could crack glass,

taps her foot in perfect time

to a life she hasn't earned.

She doesn't know what hunger is,

doesn't know what it feels like

to be swallowed by the city,

only to find it's empty

and everyone else is eating

off your bones.

I hold up my sign—

but they don't read it.

They're too busy counting their gold

and pretending they're still alive.

**ALEX TELMAN**

The coin drops

without a second thought—

just another quarter for the machine

to keep spinning

while I'm here,

just a pawn in the game

they don't even know they're playing.

The banker, the rich man in the car,

all of them—

they think their walls are high enough

to keep the world out.

But I see them,

sitting alone in their mansions,

drinking their whiskey

like it's water,

and they know—

they know they'll never be free.

Their blood is just as dirty

as mine.

The bird that flies across the sky—

he doesn't know he's chained,

flapping against the wind

like a fool thinking he's free.

I laugh,

because I know the truth.

I've seen the cage.

It's always been here.

It's everywhere.

And it's where we all end up—

waiting for the cage to close.

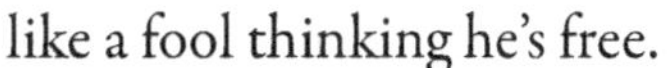

YOU THINK THEY DON'T see me, don't know I'm here, but I see them—like they're all wearing masks, like they believe they're above it all. They're strutting in their shiny shoes, their hands full of money, acting like they've earned the world, like they deserve every inch of it. Their suits look too clean, too polished. They don't even break a sweat. They just glide past me—eyes straight ahead—because if they look down, they might have to deal with the fact that they're just as hollow as I am.

But hell, I've got nothing left to hide. No illusions about who I am or what I've become. I'm here, and the world keeps turning its back on me, just like it always has. They think I don't notice. They think they can shut me out with their high walls, their shiny cars, their closed doors. But I see the cracks. I see the blood under their manicured nails, the whiskey they drink to numb the ache of knowing they're just as trapped as I am, only they don't know it yet. They don't have the courage to see it.

I laugh when I see that bird in the sky, flying so free, but he's as trapped as I am. We all are. They just don't want to face it. I'd trade places with that bird in a second, but at least I know the truth. I'm not deluded. My cage is right here, on these streets, surrounded by all the people who think they've made it. They think their money will buy them out of it. But the joke's on them.

# ALEX TELMAN

The cage isn't just made of bars—it's made of all the things we pretend to be. I can see it now, like a smog over the city. It's everywhere. And there's no escaping it—not for them, not for me. We're all just waiting for the cage to close.

# Sleeping Under the Bridge

A raw, reflective piece on sleeping rough and the humiliation of invisibility.

I SLEEP UNDER THE BRIDGE,

where the city's breath is steel and smoke,

a slow stranglehold around my neck,

the way the wind cuts through you

like a knife someone forgot to pull out.

It gnaws at your skin,

your bones—

you feel the weight of this city

before you even see it.

The bridge doesn't care,

doesn't ask for anything—

just lets me lie here,

a stray thread in its endless weave,

the concrete indifferent as a graveyard.

The hum of traffic is a lullaby

for the forgotten,

and I'm just another tired body

in the shadows,

a discarded reflection

no one bothers to look at twice.

I see them,

the ones in their suits,

tapping their shiny shoes

like it means something.

They hustle with their heads down,

like they're running toward something,

but they're just running away.

Away from the truth they're too scared to face—

that the only thing they're ever really chasing

is the edge of a cliff

they can't see yet.

And they'll fall,

just like the rest of us.

The rats?

They've got more guts than all of us—

stolen sandwiches in their claws,

eyes glittering with the hunger

that we've all forgotten to feel.

They know what it is to survive

without a goddamn plan.

They know the value of nothing.

A businessman steps over me—

no hesitation, no second thought,

just another flicker in his polished world.

But maybe he's the one who's invisible.

Maybe he's the one

who doesn't even know

he's already a corpse,

drifting through a world he's too proud to acknowledge.

Tomorrow I'll wake up—

the city's steel bones rattling above me.

I'll feel it again—the ache,

the sting of being no more than dust,

blown around like a story no one wants to tell.

But I'll still be here.

Still breathing.

Still human.

And that's what they don't get.

I'm invisible,

but I'm still here.

I'm the ghost they pretend not to see,

but I've learned to haunt this city better

than they haunt their own lives.

---

YOU WANT TO TALK ABOUT survival? You want to know what it's like to really be alive in this city? Then listen up, because this shit isn't about hope or dreams or any of that crap they sell you in movies. No, it's about lying under a bridge and feeling the wind carve its way through you like a knife. It's about hearing the hum of traffic—the same hum that's got a thousand people running in circles, thinking they're moving forward. They don't know anything. They think their shiny shoes mean they've won, but they're just rats in a fancier maze.

You see them—heads down, eyes glazed, hustling down Broadway like the city owes them something. They don't even know how empty they are. The skyscrapers they're obsessed with? They're hollow inside. Nothing but glass and steel and the lies they tell themselves every morning when they put on their ties. They walk around like they've got something important to do, but I've seen it—the misery leaking out of them. They're already dead, just haven't noticed yet. They'd never see me under the bridge, of course. Why would they? I'm just part of the background, the noise they've learned to tune out.

And you know what? I don't need them to see me. I don't need their pity or their charity. I just need to survive. I don't need a job, or a plan, or some stupid fucking dream. I need a cigarette, some dry socks, and a minute of peace in a city that doesn't give a damn if I live or die. It's not about winning here. It's about making it through another day. And that's the truth they can't handle. I'm here because the city's got nowhere else for me, but I'm still here. And that's the only victory I need.

# Skid Row Dreams

The dreams and illusions of those living on the fringes of society.

THEY CALL IT A DREAM,

this thing we chase,

but it's nothing more than a string of broken promises,

like a dog gnawing at its own tail,

round and round,

chasing the smell of something it'll never catch.

I sit here in the gutter,

watching them walk by—

the suits, the power ties,

the glossy shoes tapping out rhythms of greed.

They think they're living the dream,

but their smiles are empty as their hearts.

They move like machines,

running on the fumes of their own delusion,

believing they're better than the filth in the streets.

They see me,

but they don't see me.

Just a stain on the sidewalk,

a shadow without a name,

a forgotten page in a book no one reads.

I'm invisible in plain sight—

not even a beggar,

just a body left to rot.

No one cares to hear the stories

that spilled out of these hands

when the world turned its back.

But the rats, they know.

They know what it's like to survive,

to take what's given,

to rip it apart with your teeth

and make it yours.

I watched one today,

chewing on a sandwich someone left behind,

like it was a treasure chest.

It was living,

really living,

while the suits just kept on walking,

lost in their heads,

pretending that money means anything.

# HOMELESS IN NEW YORK

I'm not here to ask for charity.

I don't want your pity.

I just want a cigarette,

a warm bed,

something soft to touch

instead of this cold, hard pavement.

But that's not the world we live in.

You're nothing unless you've got something to sell,

something to prove,

and if you don't,

well, you're just another pile of garbage

waiting to be forgotten.

And yet, here I am.

Still breathing,

still looking up at the city that doesn't care,

thinking maybe, just maybe,

there's a crack in the concrete

where I could slip through and disappear.

But the truth is,

I'll never disappear.

I'll just keep existing—

the way shadows do,

never quite real enough

to matter.

———

I'M NOT ASKING FOR your sympathy. Don't waste your time. I've had enough of your sympathy to last a lifetime. You can throw me a dollar, give me a meal, but it won't change the truth. The truth is that I'm just a speck on the map of this city, a nothing among the millions of nows and laters, lost between the cracks of the gleaming towers that touch the sky, pretending to touch something real. These people? They walk by like I'm air. And they should. Because, to them, I am.

You think you know what's out here? You think the gutters are just gutters and the rats are just rats? No. The rats know something that you don't. They know how to survive when nothing else will. They'll rip open your trash, take what's left, chew it down, and keep going. They're not concerned with appearances. They get it. So when I watch one gnawing at a half-eaten sandwich someone threw away, I don't feel sorry for it. I envy it. The rat's living. You people? You're dying while you're still walking, with your shiny shoes and empty eyes, pretending you've made it. You're all just running in a circle, chasing a dream that died long ago.

I'm not asking for a handout. I'm just breathing in this world that doesn't give a shit. The truth is, I've learned to be invisible. And that's fine with me. It's all the same. No one's watching. No one's listening. But I keep going anyway. Why? Because I don't have a choice. You think I'm just existing here? You're wrong. I'm still alive in this shit show of a city, watching you all burn your way through your own illusions, pretending you're free. You're not. And me? I'll keep surviving, because that's what I've learned to do.

# I Have a Dream

The homeless person dreams of safety and security every night but wakes with the nightmare of death every morning

I DREAM OF DOORS THAT swing open

but only hear the sound of them slamming

again and again.

I dream of a bed,

soft and warm like the love they promised,

the love they never had to give.

I dream of a street that doesn't sneer at my shoes,

a sky that doesn't whisper death at dawn.

I dream of a world that says,

"Come,

sit,

be seen,"

but I wake to cracked pavement

and a grimy sky too tired to care.

I dream of laughing—

big belly laughs,

the kind that mean something.

The kind you forget to fake.

I dream of a bottle that isn't hollow,

a blanket that's more than just a shadow

trying to hug my skin.

But each morning,

the dream cracks open like the old man's smile

who's got nothing left but his teeth

and the rat gnawing through the cracks in the wall,

sucking on the bones of something long gone.

They told me the city would chew me up,

but they didn't tell me it would gnaw,

slow and steady,

a dull ache under the skin

like hunger I can't remember.

Like thirst in a river of poison.

I thought the dream was mine,

but it was just another trick of the light,

another dreamer selling his vision

for a dime.

I've been sold that dream—

the one where I'm not the dirt under their feet.

## HOMELESS IN NEW YORK

But every night I sleep under bridges,

and every morning

the sun rises with its back turned,

its face made of glass and steel.

And I ask:

When do I become a human again?

When do I stop being a shadow on a concrete slab

beneath a sky too busy to notice?

I don't have the answers.

They never come.

Just the cigarette butt,

the empty bottle,

the stink of piss on my boots.

But I keep moving.

Moving like the rats,

like the ghosts.

If you look closely,

you'll see me.

But you'll look away.

You always do.

HERE'S THE THING ABOUT dreams when you're on the streets: they're more like tricks. You don't get to hold them long, and even when they slip through your fingers, they're still there, haunting you, making you believe for a second you could have something real, something better. But they're lies, all of them. The dream of a bed, the warmth of a blanket, the luxury of not waking up with the taste of last night's whiskey and the stench of your own sweat. People love to sell you that dream. Hell, they sell it to themselves too. But we all wake up to the same shit.

I dream of doors that open, but those doors never do. Instead, I get the sound of them slamming shut in my face every damn morning. And the thing is, the city doesn't chew you up, it gnaws at you—slow and steady. It breaks you down a little more every day. You don't notice at first. You think you're still in the game, but then one morning you realize you've become part of the sidewalk, part of the background, just something that blends into the cracks.

I'm not asking for kindness. Hell, I don't even want your charity. I just want to be seen, even if it's just for a second. They walk by, don't even look down, and I'm just another shadow to them. Another ghost. But I'm still here, surviving the gnaw, surviving the grind.

Every night, I sleep under bridges, and every morning the sky looks down on me like I'm not even there. But I'm still moving. I keep going. Not because it matters, but because what else can you do when you've got nothing left but the will to exist?

# Coffee Shop Window

A poignant look at alienation as a homeless person gazes into the warm, bustling world inside a café.

I PRESS MY FACE TO the cold glass

and watch them—the lucky ones,

sipping their lives like they're owed,

spilling sugar on the counter

as if they believe in something sweet.

They laugh,

but the sound is empty—

like wind blowing through a broken window,

unheard, unheld,

but still full of noise.

I'm outside.

Feet frozen, fingers numb,

but their warmth,

that artificial glow,

bites harder than the cold ever could.

They sit in their worlds,

built on soft chairs and soft lies,

circling each other like planets

with no gravity,

just drifting.

They drink coffee like it's their right.

They sip it slow, like they're savoring

something that matters—

but the cup's empty,

and so are their eyes.

They don't know what hunger is.

They don't know what it's like to choke

on nothing,

to wait for a chance

that never comes.

I don't want their lives,

I don't need their soft, warm lies.

I've felt hunger like a claw,

scratching from the inside,

gnawing on the edges of what could be,

what should be.

But they wouldn't know that.

They don't look.

# HOMELESS IN NEW YORK

They just sip,

glancing out,

and their eyes pass over me

like I'm part of the sidewalk.

Invisible in a crowd

they don't see

but walk over like pavement.

I could walk in there,

order a coffee,

but they'd only look through me—

I'd be a shadow,

a stain on the glass they don't want to touch.

But maybe that's the way it's meant to be.

Maybe the glass is the barrier,

and I'm the reflection—

faded, broken,

but always staring back.

I'm what they'll never understand.

I'm the world they can't afford to see.

I press my face into the glass again,

and the heat from the café blurs

their perfect lives

until they're no more than a mirage,

shifting in the steam,

vanishing when I blink.

I'm not meant for that world.

And they're not meant for mine.

So I'll stay outside—

let the cold have me,

let the hunger burn me,

because out here, at least,

the truth is naked,

and no one can pretend

they're safe.

———————

I'M OUTSIDE. I'M ALWAYS outside, like a shadow they refuse to see. There's a warmth in there, behind the glass—warmth they drink down in between their fake laughs and their cheap dreams. I see them, those soft people with their coffee and their cushy lives, as if the world owes them something. Maybe it does. But I'm not part of that world.

I press my face to the glass and watch them live their lies, every sip of their overpriced coffee a slap in my face. They think it's real, that life. They think it means something because they have what they want, because they can sit on soft chairs in a warm café and pretend their empty words matter. But I've lived long enough to see through the walls they've built—through the layers of illusion they wrap around themselves like blankets to keep the cold away. I don't need their blankets. I need the truth, and the truth is I'm invisible to them.

I could walk in there, order a cup, but they wouldn't see me. They'd look through me like I'm nothing, a stain on their perfect little world. And maybe that's the point. Maybe the glass between us isn't just a physical barrier—it's a mirror. I'm what they refuse to look at, what they can't afford to acknowledge. I'm the truth they bury in their coffee cups and their overpriced clothes. I'm the consequence of their comfort.

But I don't need their approval. I don't need their fake smiles or their pity. I'm already living in the raw truth, the cold of it, the hunger, the noise of a world that doesn't care. The people inside that café, they have no idea what it's like to be me. And they never will.

# The Light of Times Square

A poetic meditation on how New York's bright lights contrast with the darkness of homelessness.

THE LIGHTS ARE BRASH tonight,

pounding like a drum in my chest,

but I'm out here in the dark,

waiting for the heat to slip through the cracks of my coat

like all the things I'm not.

A dream in motion,

caught between the steel jaws of this city

and the smoke in my lungs.

I watch them,

those suited ghosts that pass by with their heads down,

rushing past the neon circus,

their eyes fixed on nothing,

like they think this place—this broken light—

will somehow make them more than they are.

But I know,

I know the truth—

# HOMELESS IN NEW YORK

this city chews you up

and spits you out like an empty can,

then it moves on to the next one.

No mercy.

No second chances.

I see the café windows lit up,

people wrapped in warmth and conversation

like they've all got somewhere to be,

but there's nowhere for me.

No seat at the table.

I'm a shadow in a place full of ghosts,

caught between the lines of their laughter

and the sour breath of the street.

It's funny—

they'll never see me,

but I'm part of the show.

The way I drag my bones through the gutter,

the way I watch their lives unfold

like cheap TV shows they'll forget by morning.

The bright lights above me

are a lie,

a flickering lie

that keeps me moving,

keeps me pretending I'm not alone.

But they don't know.

They're just a few steps away

from where I am.

Sometimes I wonder if the city's made of the same stuff as me—

broken dreams and unfinished promises,

streets that stretch forever

but never lead anywhere.

Maybe we're all just waiting,

waiting for something we'll never see.

That bright, warm future that doesn't come,

not for me,

not for anyone who's ever been forgotten.

They don't know the price of their light.

They think it's free,

that it's a gift,

a reward for doing things right.

But I see through the illusion,

the glass,

the smoke,

the sound of footsteps

that get lost in the roar of the city.

I am the silence between the noise,

the breath held tight

before the inevitable fall.

Maybe they'll remember me one day,

maybe they won't.

Maybe that's the point.

In this city,

no one is ever really gone

until they've been swallowed whole.

And so I walk,

no destination in mind—

just the next block,

the next shadow,

the next cigarette

to keep the hunger at bay

for one more hour.

I am the dark behind the lights,

the echo no one wants to hear.

I am the space between the stars,

the afterthought of a dream

that was never mine to begin with.

But the lights keep shining,

and I keep moving

through the gaps

they leave behind.

———————

THE LIGHTS IN TIMES Square—they burn bright, don't they? Like a sick joke that keeps flashing in your face, telling you that if you just keep looking, something good will happen. But it's all smoke and mirrors. I watch them—those people in their coats, their suits, their shiny faces. They're in a hurry, like they're on the clock. But what do they really have? A shiny pair of shoes, maybe. Some good coffee in their bellies. A future they think they own. They pass me like I'm nothing—like I'm some detail on the sidewalk, something to step over, something to ignore.

I watch them, not because I want to. Hell, I'm not some voyeur. But I can't help it. They're warm. They're real. They're part of that world I'll never touch, never belong to. They walk in a kind of rhythm, like they know where they're going, like they're not lost. Like they've got a map to the future and I'm just a faded line in the corner of the page. But I don't have that map. I don't have a future. What I have is a cigarette burning down to the filter, a half-empty stomach, and a dream that never comes true.

The lights flicker and I get lost in them. But there's nothing warm in their glow for me. No seat at their table. I'm stuck out here in the cold, a ghost in the city's belly, listening to them laugh and talk like they're part of some better version of life. But I know, deep down, that it's just as hollow as this cracked sidewalk I'm lying on. It doesn't matter how high the lights get or how loud the noise. They don't see me. They never will. And maybe that's the real darkness.

# The Train Car Symphony

The experience of traveling on the subway and finding unexpected communion with strangers.

THE TRAIN SCREECHES its metallic hymns,

rattling the soul like a prayer forgotten—

a hollow song that doesn't care if anyone listens.

I'm staring out, nose pressed to glass,

the city outside a flood of lights and shadows,

so many voices, so many faces

that don't even know I'm here.

She's in the designer jacket,

perfect shoes,

the world spinning at her feet like it owes her something.

She doesn't see me,

or the man asleep next to the door,

his crumpled jacket like a discarded memory.

But I see them all.

I see the way her eyes flicker to the phone screen

and think of a thousand things I could say—

but won't.

I see the cracks in the pavement she steps on

and think about how I have nowhere else to go,

nothing to hold,

just the flicker of my own breath

in this steel beast.

A child laughs in the corner—

a brief, sharp sound that cuts through the noise—

so pure it almost breaks me.

The laugh fades, swallowed

by the hum of this metallic tomb.

And I wonder if he'll grow up

to forget what it feels like to be

in the belly of the city

where nothing's free but the air that tastes like rust.

I'm breathing it all in—

the air thick with sweat,

old perfume,

and the scent of a hundred lost souls

floating,

fading into the sound of the wheels

clanging like the echoes of a thousand forgotten prayers.

# HOMELESS IN NEW YORK

This place is an orchestra of loneliness,

every voice a broken note,

every step a drumbeat for the damned.

I fit right in.

The light hits the rails

like a revelation no one wants to hear,

and I think of the man asleep by the door,

his hand twitching like he's dreaming of something better,

someplace where the trains don't go.

I watch them all—

the ones who walk in the city like it's their home,

like it owes them something.

They rush toward it,

pushing past me

like I'm nothing more than a stain

on the windows they never clean.

But I'm part of it.

The city and I,

we're the same—

gritty, worn down,

too much pain and not enough love.

The lights up there?

They don't shine for me.

But hell, they don't shine for her either.

They just burn and burn

until you can't tell the difference

between the soul and the sweat.

And when the train stops,

I'll get off.

But for now,

I'm here—

in this rhythm of iron,

in this fading song,

waiting for the city to remember me.

For just a second.

Before it forgets again.

───────────────

YOU THINK YOU SEE ME. You think you understand. You look at me and decide I'm the invisible man, the one who doesn't count. But I'm not invisible, not really. I'm here. I'm breathing the same air you breathe, but we don't share the same world. You step onto the subway, your polished shoes tap on the floor, and your mind is somewhere far away, or maybe it's just on the next thing—work, family, whatever the hell you're chasing. You don't even notice the guy leaning against the door, his jacket frayed from too many nights on concrete. You don't see the weight in his eyes that says he's lost everything but still carries it all with him.

You're too busy with your thoughts, your plans, your safe little life. But me? I see you. I see everything about you. I see the hunger in your rush, the loneliness you try to cover up with your shiny facade. And I laugh. I laugh because you think you're free. You think those lights above the train are there to show you the way. They're not. They're just another distraction—blinding you to what's really happening.

This train car is my symphony, my stage, and you're all just actors pretending not to notice the orchestra of despair that plays under your feet. Each screech, each rattle, is a note in a song you don't hear. But me? I hear it. And I know you hear it too, you just drown it out with your headphones, your chatter, your self-righteous distractions.

I'm not asking for your sympathy. I'm not asking for your help. I'm just here. I'm a reminder that you, too, could be a moment away from everything falling apart. And when that happens, don't look at me and think I'm the one who failed. You might end up just like me, looking out the window, wishing for something more.

# Central Park at Night

The beauty and danger of the park after dark for someone without a home.

THE TREES ARE GIANTS in the fog,

their limbs clawing at the moon—

a slow-motion waltz between branches and light,

and I'm sitting on a bench

too tired to be afraid,

too cold to care.

The park's beauty is a beast.

A smile for the lost—

but it isn't real.

The shadows spill over

like ink on a too-thin page,

soaking the ground until

there's nothing left but

the smell of wet concrete,

the flickering streetlights.

I watch the rats scurry

like they've got somewhere to be,

but nowhere to go.

I see them move through the cracks,

under the benches where

my hands grip the wood

like a prayer.

Maybe the night's a promise,

maybe it's a lie.

Maybe it's just the sound of something,

somewhere, in the distance—

a light burning somewhere

on the other side of the world.

But it won't ever reach me here.

I've forgotten what it means to belong.

To feel the warmth of a hand,

the touch of something human.

I've forgotten the taste of food

that wasn't stolen

or scavenged from the ground.

They tell me there's hope—

but hope is like a cloud.

It hangs there,

but you can't touch it.

I close my eyes,

and the park whispers

its secrets—

nothing to say,

nothing to offer.

I wonder,

if I disappear into this night,

will anyone notice?

Will they stop for a second,

look at the space where I was,

and wonder if I was ever real?

Or will they just walk past

the shadows I leave behind?

---

THE THING ABOUT CENTRAL Park at night is it doesn't give a damn. The trees reach up into the sky, but they don't care if you're here or not. They stand like silent witnesses to the way this world goes. People walk by with their heads held high, as if the city's lights were made for them, as if they own every shadow in the street. I sit here in the dark, the cold gnawing at my bones, and it's like the park itself is telling me, "Yeah, you're here, but you're not here." It's not a place for the forgotten; it's just a place, like any other. A place that doesn't ask, doesn't care.

I've lost track of how many nights I've slept here, how many bottles I've counted in the gutter, how many stars I've stared at like they had answers to give. But they don't. The lights of the city burn like a lie you keep telling yourself until it tastes real. You look up and think, "If I could just get there, I'd be something." But that's the problem. You get there, and it's still the same. Nothing but a flash in the distance that never really shines on you.

I watch the rats because they've got something I don't: movement. They're always going somewhere, always running, always hiding. But me? I'm stuck. Stuck in this night where every streetlight is a dream that's too far to touch. Maybe I've been here too long to care, or maybe it's the other way around—I've stopped caring because I've been here too long.

And I know, deep down, that when I'm gone, there won't be a moment of silence for me. There won't be anyone asking, "What happened to him?" Because that's not how the world works. It just moves on, dragging everyone along with it.

# The City That Never Sleeps, and Neither Do I

The existential connection between the endless energy of New York and the restless, sleepless mind of the homeless.

THE CITY HUMS ITS NEON promise.

lights flicker like desperate gamblers

chasing a win they'll never collect.

The towers scream—

we're open,

we're on,

we're always here—

but they've forgotten to tell me

they're empty inside.

It's a loop,

a wheel spinning faster than I can breathe,

and I'm left standing in the middle

of this circus,

looking up,

waiting for the next act to start,

but nothing ever happens.

## HOMELESS IN NEW YORK

The streetlights bleed into the pavement,

burning holes in the concrete,

the shadows of a million strangers

passing,

sliding by with their heads down,

minds full of numbers

and plans

I don't care to understand.

They walk in rhythm,

but I'm stuck in the static,

wondering where the noise ends

and the silence begins.

I sit on a cracked bench,

under the last breath of daylight,

my mind buzzing louder than the trains,

my body aching in ways I can't name.

The city doesn't stop,

but neither do I.

I'm part of the pulse,

a glitch in the system,

the missing piece

no one's looking for.

Somewhere, in the dark,

someone's watching me—

maybe pitying me,

maybe just passing through

like the rest.

But I don't need their pity,

don't need their prayers

or their coins.

I need the city to stop for a second,

just one second,

to let me breathe

in the same air

they're breathing.

But it never does.

So I sit.

And wait.

And listen.

To the beat of the street.

The city hums.

And neither of us sleeps.

THE CITY'S GOT ITS lights on, always on, but what's the use? You think the lights are there for me? They shine down like they're gods, but I'm the one left in the dirt, in the shadow of them, trying to catch my breath between the cracks. They don't stop, they never stop. I've seen it—people rushing, heads down, racing to some invisible finish line that doesn't care if I'm here or not. They think they're important, like their lives mean more, but you can feel it—there's something broken in all that movement. I don't need their sympathy, hell no. I'm not a cause, I'm not a number for some charity to check off their list. I'm a reminder. A reminder of how far they've fallen, even if they don't see it. They move like they're all busy, like they're full of meaning, and I'm left to sit in the gutter, in the dark. But I hear them. Their shoes on the pavement, their voices muffled under the hum of the city. They're living, they're breathing—but are they really alive?

I'm part of the city's pulse, like it or not. I feel it. The rush, the noise, the endless thrum. But I'm not part of what they call living. I'm the part they ignore, the part that falls off the track and gets kicked to the side. But I don't mind. There's something free about it, something real about being the last one to matter. I sit on that bench and watch them, watch them all chasing their dreams. They'll never stop, not for me. But I don't need them to. I need the city to stop for a second, to breathe with me, just for one damn minute. But it won't. And neither will I.

# Empty Bottles, Empty Stomachs

A focus on substance abuse, self-destruction, and the physical toll of homelessness.

THE BOTTLES PILE UP

like hollow teeth.

I suck on their emptiness

as if it could fill

the hole in my chest,

but it just gets deeper—

the bottle's cold kiss

burns like an old lover

who never really cared,

and I chase her down anyway.

I've seen the sun rise

and thought maybe I'd made it,

but each morning is just

a reminder of how it's all

slipping through my fingers,

like sand and piss.

# HOMELESS IN NEW YORK

the streets hum a lullaby

that don't put me to sleep.

I've learned the rhythm

of every bottle,

its weight, its clink.

a song of rust,

but I'm still awake.

empty bottles, empty stomachs—

there's a hunger in us

bigger than the streets,

bigger than the hunger

that chews at the insides.

we're all starving for something,

but it's never enough.

I drink it all down,

but the ache keeps coming back.

it don't stop.

not until the night comes crawling,

quiet like a thief

who's taken everything.

and when I close my eyes,

I see it again—

the next bottle.

the next shot.

the next night

I'll drink myself to sleep

and wake up still here,

still hungry,

still empty.

but maybe it's just

the way the world

keeps spinning—

empty bottles

and empty stomachs

all the way down.

———————

YEAH, I SEE YOU LOOKIN' at me like I'm some kind of mistake. Some lost cause, wandering around with a bottle in my hand and nothing but a body to drag behind me. But you don't get it, do you? This bottle ain't my savior. It's just a thing to hold me over, to numb the fire that keeps eating me from the inside. It's not even about the alcohol anymore—it's about the chase, the hunger. That pit in my gut that never goes away. The ache that's always there, gnawing, relentless, like the fucking streets themselves.

I chase that cold kiss because it's the closest thing to love I'll ever get. And you don't know that feeling—that desperate, empty kind of love, the one where you know they don't care but you keep coming back anyway. It's a rhythm, you see? I've learned it. The bottle, the weight, the sound it makes when I crack it open. It's like music to me now, the sound of something breaking and filling the silence. The streets hum a lullaby too, but it doesn't put me to sleep. It's just noise. Constant, like the hunger.

You think I want this? You think I don't see the sun rise and feel it all slipping away, like sand running through my fingers? The world keeps spinning, keeps going, but I stay stuck in this hole, chasing after something that can't fill it. I drink myself to sleep, but it's just a pause. When I wake up, I'm still here. Still hungry. Still empty. But I keep drinking, keep looking for something to stop the ache, even though I know it'll never be enough.

Empty bottles, empty stomachs. That's all we are. Just hungry ghosts, wandering through the nights, waiting for the next bottle to show us a way out that doesn't exist.

# Empty Bottles, Empty Stomachs pt2

You think I don't know?

You think I don't feel it—

the way those empty bottles stack up,

the way they rattle their damn bones

like they're waiting for me to fill them,

like they're the ones that can save me.

But they can't.

They never have.

You look at me like I'm a ghost,

but ghosts don't hurt.

They don't bleed,

don't wake up to the same damn street every morning,

same puddle of piss,

same buzz from a bottle that doesn't hit right anymore.

You think it's about the booze?

It's not.

It's about the hollow.

The fucking black hole inside me

that never stops asking for more.

## HOMELESS IN NEW YORK

You ever starve for something you can't name?

That gnawing hunger,

the one that don't stop when you swallow.

I've swallowed a lot—

a lot of shit,

a lot of pain,

a lot of liquor.

And it doesn't fill it.

Doesn't fill me.

And you think I don't know what that means?

I know.

More than you ever will.

But there's no stopping, is there?

No rest for a man who's already dead.

A man who wakes up every day

thinking today will be the day

he doesn't have to reach for the next bottle.

But that day never comes.

This is me.

And these empty bottles,

they're all that's left.

I'll drink 'em dry,

and maybe tomorrow

I'll wake up again

and do it all over.

Because at least I know how it goes.

At least I can count on that.

---

SO, YOU LOOK AT ME, like I'm invisible—like I'm some stray that wandered too far off course, and now I'm nothing but a shadow in the corners of your world. But you don't get it. You think you know, but you don't. You don't know what it's like to wake up to the same cracked street every damn morning, to feel the same hunger gnawing at your insides, a hunger that no meal, no drink, no damn thing can touch.

You look at my bottles like they're the problem, but they're just my company. Those empty rattling ghosts are the only thing left that makes any noise in this silence. They sit there like a pile of broken promises, waiting for me to fill them up, to believe that one more sip will fix what's broken inside me. But they don't. They never do.

You think it's about the booze, about the buzz, but it's not. It's the fucking hole. The abyss inside me that screams louder than anything you can imagine. I've swallowed it all—my pain, my regrets, my failures, my self-destruction—and still, the hunger won't stop. You've never starved for something you can't name. You can't understand that gnawing, aching emptiness that no one and nothing can touch.

But you think I'm lost? Hell, maybe I am. But there's no stopping. No end to this cycle. No day where I'll wake up and say, "today's the day." Because I know that day's a lie. I'll wake up, same as always, reach for the bottle, and do it again. At least I know how it goes. At least I have that. So yeah, you think I don't know? Well, I know more than you ever will.

# Lost in the Streets of Brooklyn

The feeling of displacement in a borough known for its constant reinvention and gentrification.

I WANDER THESE STREETS like a ghost who forgot to die,

Brooklyn's skin stretching,

changing,

gentrifying its bones for the rich,

burying the rest of us under the weight of progress.

Who am I now?

The world reboots every week,

but I stay stuck in a loop,

walking the same cracked sidewalks,

passing the same closed bars,

the same golden window displays,

while I'm eating yesterday's leftovers

and hoping the rats didn't already pick them clean.

You can't breathe here.

There's no air for men like me—

too much money,

too much hustle,

too many of them,

too few of us.

I watch the skyline rise like a church,

praying for salvation.

It's got no love for me,

no room for a man whose skin's too worn

and heart's too heavy.

Who am I here?

Just a blur,

a shadow in the corner of a storefront,

fading every minute

like the last drink in an empty bottle.

I've seen the condos spring from the rubble

like weeds in the cracks of a broken sidewalk.

The faces change,

the names change,

the rent changes,

but I'm still the same—

still the lost one,

still the ghost.

I wear my past like a coat that's too tight,

and the people who walk by don't see it.

They walk over me like I'm part of the pavement,

like I'm just another crack

they don't need to fix.

They say Brooklyn's alive,

but I can't feel it.

I can't feel a damn thing.

Just the rumble of trains beneath my feet,

the clink of bottles I drink to drown out the noise,

the laughter that echoes from behind locked doors

I'll never enter.

They've remade this place a thousand times

and forgotten every face that didn't fit.

And I'm still here,

watching the parade go by,

wondering if maybe—just maybe—

they'll look back,

but they never do.

This street—

this dying Brooklyn—

has no love for me.

It's only got space for the next shiny thing.

And I'm just the ghost that haunts its past.

———

I'VE WALKED THESE STREETS for so long they've stopped feeling like streets—more like a prison I built with my own two hands, one brick at a time. Brooklyn's reinvented itself so many times, I can't keep up. They turn the old bars into condos, the corner shops into overpriced boutiques. All that history, all that struggle—it's just background noise now, part of a soundtrack that nobody listens to anymore. They've traded their sweat for silver, their soul for property value, and I'm left here, a ghost, fading into the concrete.

I see them pass by, walking fast, all dressed up in the latest shit, living their lives like they own this place, like they've always belonged here. But they don't see me. They don't see the way the streets chew you up and spit you out. They don't know what it's like to wake up in the same puddle of piss you fell asleep in, to stretch your bones and realize the only thing you can count on is the cold air in your lungs.

They think I'm invisible, but I know better. I'm not invisible; I'm just ignored. That's the hardest part. The not being seen. I'm just another part of the scenery—another homeless man to step over, another face to avoid. Brooklyn's a place for the rich, for the shiny, for the new. It doesn't have room for me. I'm yesterday's news in a city that only wants tomorrow.

I'll keep walking, though. Keep moving. Keep watching the skyline get taller while I stay smaller. There's no redemption here. No salvation. Just the same dirty street corners and the clink of bottles, hoping the next one will bring me peace, even though I know it won't. But what else is there? At least I'm here. At least I'm still breathing. Barely.

# The Forgotten Faces of Harlem

Homelessness in a neighborhood that's historically been a cultural heartbeat for Black Americans.

THEY'RE KNOCKING DOWN everything—

the old brick and bone,

the rhythm of our streets

cracking like dried skin.

You can't hear it,

but the bones scream,

bodies displaced by glass towers—

condos rise like tumors,

disease creeping in where history bled.

You think we don't see?

You think we don't feel the change—

the old blues, the jazz,

fading into air like smoke,

swallowed up by sterile walls,

replaced with the hum of corporate veins

pumping white noise into the arteries.

They dress the city up

and call it progress,

but all I see are ghosts

who never left,

still hanging like curses

in the windows of buildings that don't care.

What do you do when the city

you bled for, bled into,

turns its back on you?

What do you do when Harlem

becomes a name on a plaque

instead of a pulse?

The corners where we bled

are now Instagram hotspots—

soul for sale,

as if nothing ever mattered

except what can be sold.

I'm still here,

shuffling through the wreckage

of my own memory,

wondering if I can hold on

before I'm swallowed by the dust

of these empty streets.

They say a neighborhood dies

when its ghosts stop fighting,

but we never stopped—

we've just been made invisible,

like we were always meant to be.

And they can knock down the buildings,

but they'll never touch the ground

we bled into,

the ground that knows our names.

And I'm still waiting for the hour

when the city will remember

what it's forgotten,

when Harlem can rise from its ashes

like a song that doesn't fade.

Until then,

I'll keep walking these streets

with the ghosts,

because they never left.

They never will.

YOU THINK YOU'VE SEEN it all, but you don't know what it feels like to have the city chew you up and spit you out—like gum on the sidewalk that nobody bothers to scrape off. You walk through Harlem now, don't you? All shiny and new, with your condos and your fancy boutiques, and you don't even notice me sitting on the corner, buried beneath layers of history and neglect. But you notice the "progress," don't you? The ones who turned their backs on the ones who built this city, the ones who bled into these streets—those faces, the real faces, now just whispers in the wind. Harlem's gone, replaced by something with a prettier face, a cleaner street, and a higher rent.

You'll never see what's really happening here. You'll never feel the way the bricks still hum with the ghosts of the past, the beat of the drum that built this place—slowly being washed away like the piss in the alley behind you. But I feel it. It's in my bones. This was my home once. Hell, this was everyone's home. And now? Now it's just another set of glass windows, another overpriced apartment with a skyline view, and they can put all the paint they want on it—they'll never erase the blood we spilled here.

You look at me like I'm nothing, like I'm invisible, but I'm still here. The only thing they can't steal is the ground we stood on, the ground that saw our rise and our fall. They think I'm gone, that I've disappeared into the cracks, but they're wrong. I'm here. And when this city finally wakes up, it'll remember us, even if it doesn't want to. They can knock down the buildings, but they can't kill the truth of what was here. We're still here, in the rubble, in the silence, in the ghosts.

# Begging for a Dollar, But No One Sees

The invisibility of homelessness and the psychological toll it takes on a person's dignity.

I HOLD OUT MY HAND,

a tired paper cup,

waiting for crumbs of their pity—

but I am invisible.

A shadow,

I slip through the cracks of their world,

where feet click on the pavement,

and eyes glide past,

never catching what's left of me.

I smell of piss,

of sweat and yesterday's news,

but they don't know what that means—

how many nights

have passed with the same smell,

how many days I've begged for the noise of a coin

to crack the silence

like a bullet through glass.

They look at me,

and I am a stain

on their shiny city,

a crack in their perfect mirrors.

But it's not me they fear.

It's the hunger that crawls beneath their skin,

the one they refuse to acknowledge.

I shake,

and they turn away.

I beg,

and they move faster.

They want to believe

this could never be them,

never be their bones exposed,

their hearts scoured by the weight of nothing.

I ask for a dollar—

just one.

But the world's full of ghosts,

and I am one of them now.

I don't need their pity.

I need the recognition

that I've been here

longer than they've lived

in their sterile, glass towers.

I watch their faces

as they pass me by,

shift from clean to dirty,

like reflections in a cracked window.

They don't know me,

but I see them—

all their tired dreams and cold stares.

And I wonder,

when they look at me,

do they see their own fear?

The emptiness they refuse to face,

the hunger they swallow down

and never speak of?

I beg for a dollar,

but my soul's price is higher than their guilt.

Still, I hold my hand out—

maybe tomorrow,

they'll see me.

Maybe tomorrow,

they'll care.

----

THEY WALK PAST ME LIKE I'm nothing. Hell, they treat me like I'm air,

like I'm a ghost just lingering between the cracks of their perfect lives. I

hold my cup out, not to beg, not to beg for scraps, but to be seen. That's

the problem, you see—they don't look. I'm not invisible to me, but to

them, I'm just another shadow they have to ignore, another reminder

that their shiny little world could fall apart in a heartbeat.

I could stand here all day, my bones aching, my stomach gnawing,

watching their eyes slide over me like I'm some stain on their shoes.

They can't stand still long enough to even hear the scrape of my voice,

the scratch of hunger in my throat. They think they're better than me,

but I'm just one bad break from wearing that same suit they wear,

one lost paycheck from sitting in their plush office chair,

staring out their glass windows wondering how fast their soul can

decompose in a life they don't even want.

I ask for a dollar, but it's not about the money. It's about the silence.

It's about the way they've built their lives with so many walls,

they can't even see a person standing right in front of them. I don't

need a dime from them—I need them to see. To recognize I'm here,

that I have a name, that I matter. I matter more than their bullshit,

more than the story they tell themselves at night, curled up in their heated beds.

Tomorrow, I'll ask again. Maybe they'll look. Maybe they won't.

But I'll be here, holding my cup out, waiting for someone

to finally see what's been standing right in front of them all along.

# The Stench of the Subway Grate

The stench of the city as a metaphor for societal neglect and the scents of despair.

THE CITY SPITS ITS soul through the grate,

a fetid breath that clings to everything,

the concrete skin sweating

and peeling beneath the weight of its own lies.

they walk around like ghosts,

heads down, eyes straight,

passing over the bodies

that are too tired to rise.

the stench isn't just piss and rot—

it's the smell of every promise broken

by someone who thought the world owed them something.

you drop a coin in my cup,

like that makes a difference,

but you've already forgotten my face

before your feet leave the pavement.

don't look at me too long,

**HOMELESS IN NEW YORK**

I'll remind you of things

you don't want to remember.

I'll make you feel your guilt,

the guilt of the city you love

but never see.

I'm just one more stain

on your carefully curated skyline.

I used to have a name,

a place to lay my head,

but now I'm nothing but a shadow,

a crack in the pavement.

you pass by like I'm invisible,

but I'm here,

my bones too heavy for the air.

I can hear your footsteps

get louder as you get closer,

then silence

as you cross the street

to avoid the truth of me.

the stench isn't the air,

it's the weight of you ignoring it,

of turning away,

of pretending you can't smell

the rot that's been seeping through

for years.

this city doesn't care.

it never cared.

it just keeps moving forward,

like a rat chasing the cheese

it'll never taste.

═══════════

THEY WALK BY ME EVERY day. Heads up, eyes down, pretending they don't see me—pretending they don't smell me. The city spits its filth on me, and I wear it like a badge. It's a stench, yeah, but it's more than piss and rotting food. It's the scent of people who forgot how to care. I'm part of the pavement, part of the noise they filter out of their lives. I've got a face, sure, but you wouldn't know it because I'm invisible. You drop a coin in my cup, then forget I exist before the sound of your footsteps fades. That coin doesn't fix anything. It doesn't fix me. It doesn't fix this world that's gone bad, rotten at the core. You all walk around with your shiny little worlds, your coffee cups and your designer bags, looking at me like I'm something that happened to someone else. You can't even look me in the eye. You can't stand the truth of what I represent.

I used to be someone. I had a name, a place to sleep at night, a home. But the city took that away, chewed it up and spit it out like the empty bottle I leave by the curb. I'm just another shadow, another stain on your perfect city. And you avoid me like I'll rub off on you. Well, maybe I will. Maybe that's the problem—you're scared I'll remind you of who you really are when no one's watching. When all the pretty masks come off. This isn't about money, or the handouts you think you've given me. It's about seeing me. About not pretending I'm invisible just because you want to keep your nice little world clean. It's about the rot you've built your city on. And you can smell it. You just don't want to admit it.

# A Bed of Newspaper and Dreams

A meditation on makeshift homes, the illusion of security, and the fragile nature of human survival.

THE CITY DOESN'T SLEEP

but I do—

pressed against the grate,

tucked into a bed of shredded newsprint,

ink-stained sheets that peel away

with every gust of wind

like promises that never made it.

they walk over me—

briefcase and heels clicking,

they don't see the broken man

swallowed by his own despair,

the jagged edges of humanity

brushing past me

like the forgotten pages of a book

nobody wants to read.

I was once a man

# HOMELESS IN NEW YORK

with dreams in my pockets—

dreams that fit snug

against the ribs,

a tight bundle of hope

that danced on the edge of hunger,

but it's been years

and now I have nothing

but the smell of exhaust

and piss soaked into my skin,

the sickly sweet stench of society's leftovers.

I used to laugh—

a man needs a laugh, right?

but now it's just a whisper,

a wheeze from a hollow chest

that has no place to call home.

the rats have taken more

than my pride—

they've claimed my dignity,

scratching at the edges of my sanity

like gnawing teeth on soft wood.

I can feel them,

tiny devils crawling,

watching me sleep

with their beady eyes,

as I lie here on this pile of dead newspapers,

wishing for just one more chance

to make the world believe

I'm more than this,

more than the smell of sweat and decay,

more than the rusted bones

of a forgotten man.

but the city doesn't care—

it doesn't even blink.

people rush by like shadows,

the hum of trains and the screech of tires

covering the silence

of a life being erased.

the newspaper rustles

like a lover's last kiss,

the ink bleeding into my skin

as I close my eyes,

fighting to hold onto a memory

of what it felt like

to be human.

nobody sees me—

they never do—

except for the rats

who come out at night,

their tiny hearts beating

to the rhythm of the train,

that black metal beast

that carries everyone

but me.

———————————

I SLEEP UNDER THE GRATE, in the shadows where the city forgets you, where the wind cuts through the seams of the makeshift bed I've crafted from shredded newspapers. They're my sheets now, ink-stained, torn to pieces, but what the hell else am I supposed to use? You can't pick up a blanket on the street—people hoard their comforts like they're the last scraps of something precious. So, I've got this, this pile of old papers that nobody reads, ink smudged into my skin like a tattoo nobody asked for.

The city doesn't sleep, but I do. I don't have the luxury to stay awake, not with the cold seeping into my bones. The hum of the subway, the noise of the streets, the click of heels above me—all of it drowns out the sound of my own thoughts. They walk right over me, like I'm not even here, like I don't even exist. They're too busy with their shiny shoes and their briefcases, thinking they've got it all figured out, thinking their lives mean something more than mine. But I'm not invisible to the rats. They see me. They come out at night, tiny devils that gnaw away at my dignity, at my sanity. They don't care that I'm a person. I'm just a bed for them to crawl across, a spot to rest their little claws.

I wasn't always like this. I didn't always wake up to the stench of exhaust and piss. I wasn't always just another broken man pressed into the corner of a street, swallowed whole by the city. I had dreams once—dreams that sat close to my chest, snug between my ribs, where they'd stay warm and safe. I had something to hold onto. I didn't always feel like I was being eaten alive from the inside out. But years go by, and those dreams slip away, one at a time, until all that's left is this. The stink of the world that doesn't care about me. The hunger. The cold. The rats.

They don't see me. They never do. The people who pass by don't know the sound of my laugh because I haven't heard it in years. A man needs to laugh, but I forgot how to. It's just a whisper now, a wheeze, the sound of a man too tired to pretend he's still human. The streets don't care about me, and neither do they.

I used to think maybe I could make something out of this, make them see me, make them understand that I'm more than this pile of rags and piss-soaked newsprint. But the city doesn't blink. It doesn't care. People rush past, their heads down, lost in their own worlds. They don't even notice the man in the gutter, the one who once had something more than this. They don't see the way my bones rattle with every gust of wind, the way my skin burns from the cold, the way my stomach clenches from hunger.

I wish they'd see me. I wish they'd stop for just a second, look me in the eyes, and understand that I was someone too. That I had a life, that I had purpose once. But there's no time for that. There's no time for the forgotten ones in a city that eats its own. There's no time for someone like me, someone who doesn't fit into the picture they've painted of this place.

I'm just here. I don't know how long I've been here. I don't know if I'll ever leave. But the city, it doesn't care. It doesn't even notice me. I'm just another broken man lying in the gutter. A memory that's long been erased.

# Chasing Shadows on Wall Street

The economic divide in New York, and the search for shadows of hope among the city's towering skyscrapers.

THE CITY EATS ITS OWN.

It chews the bones of men

who forgot how to fight back,

who mistook silence for strength,

their eyes hollow,

like empty bottles

left to collect dust.

A homeless man,

his hair a bird's nest of wires,

chews on half-bread, half-dream—

searching for a coin

that will never find his pocket,

listening for footsteps

that never stop for him.

The sky's already dead,

folded into itself

like an old newspaper

no one bothers to read.

The towers rise,

teeth white as god's lie,

chewing the air

and spitting out the rest of us.

A broker moves by,

his soul wrapped in silk

and stained with greed,

his hand trembling

but not from hunger—

he's scared of nothing,

except what's inside him—

a machine that feeds on dreams

until the last one dies in his chest.

The kid with the sign—

"Will work for food"—

stands frozen,

eyes wide,

not from hope,

but from the knowledge

that hope here is a currency,

a thing to buy and sell.

He looks up

at the digital grin of success

flashing across a billboard,

and knows—

he's not part of this game.

He's already lost,

but the rules were never his to play.

I've seen this city eat itself—

a snake that swallows its own tail,

its hunger endless,

its belly never full.

It feeds you slow,

gnaws at your soul

with the precision of a surgeon,

cutting away the parts

that once meant something—

your dignity,

your dreams,

your name.

The pigeons know it, too—

they peck at the crumbs

we leave behind,

they shit on our marble steps

and never get punished for it.

They know how to survive

in a world that's too cold

to care.

The shadows stretch long across Wall Street—

they're not just shadows,

they're promises,

and promises are hungry.

They reach for your throat,

sharp as knives,

thicker than any dollar bill

you'll ever fold in your pocket.

The city hums,

but it doesn't sing.

It groans,

like the last breath of a dying man

who never got to say goodbye.

Its voice is the sound of money

sloshing in the pockets of the rich,

the sound of a heart

beating out its final notes

to the rhythm of greed.

I thought I'd find something here—

a spark, a glimmer,

a place to breathe

without the weight of history on my chest.

But this city,

this city doesn't make room for men

who still remember how to dream.

It swallows them whole,

chews them up,

spits them out into the streets

like broken toys

the market no longer needs.

And so I chase the shadows,

because they're the only thing still moving,

the only thing left

that hasn't been bought

or sold.

But even shadows die here.

The last train comes,

but there's nowhere to go—

no place where the light doesn't feel

like a lie.

The city's full of ghosts,

but it doesn't care to remember

their names.

They wander,

looking for a door

that will never open.

And I walk with them,

because I know,

deep inside,

I'm already one of them—

just another shadow

waiting to fade away.

Maybe that's the only truth here:

this city doesn't cast shadows.

It eats them.

And we're all just waiting

for the hunger to come for us.

———————————

YOU THINK YOU KNOW what it's like, don't you? You see me sitting there, ragged and wasted, eyes glazed over like I've lost the will to care. You walk by, pretending not to notice. That's the game we play. You with your fancy clothes and your clean hands, acting like you've got it all figured out. You don't. You're just one step away from where I am. But you can't see that, can you?

They keep telling me I'm invisible, but I've never been harder to see. I'm here, aren't I? Flesh and bone, breathing, hurting. But you can't see me for what I am. You see the dirt, the rags, the bottle in my hand, but you don't see the mind that's still working, the heart that's still beating, the soul that's still clinging to some shred of something. You just step over me, walk past me, like I'm part of the city's forgotten trash. But you've forgotten something too, haven't you? You've forgotten how close you are to this. The system, that cold thing up there in the towers, the same one that spits you out once you're no longer useful, it's the same thing that keeps me in the dirt. We're both just numbers to them. Just a cog in the machine. Only difference is, you still think you're running it.

They've got their golden lives, their overpriced coffee, their plush offices. But I've seen the hunger in their eyes, haven't you? You think they're not scared? They're scared, alright. Scared of me. Scared of what could happen if they slip. Scared of becoming like me. So they bury their heads in their work, because they know, deep down, that they've got no more control over this world than I do. The only difference is, they're too proud to admit it.

**The Grit of the Lower East Side** (Final Version)

- The mix of art, poverty, culture, and survival on this historically gritty and vibrant side of the city.

———————————

THE STREETS SMELL LIKE piss,

stale ambition, and ghost stories

no one's bothered to tell.

The cracked sidewalk grinds its teeth,

swallowing the night,

a thousand broken bottles whisper

the names of the damned,

of the ones who never made it.

A man with no name

shakes his tin cup,

fingers stiff, skin like old paper—

waiting for you to look,

waiting for the pity

that never comes.

His eyes are maps of ruins,

veins like cracked highways

leading nowhere.

He doesn't know where to go—

he doesn't care anymore.

He just wants you to see him,

for one second,

to know that he's still here.

That's all.

That's all.

The buildings bend like they're trying to get away—

windows cracked like a thousand mouths

begging for something, anything,

to stop the bleeding.

And still, the city hums its tired song—

the screech of metal,

the boom of engines,

the slam of doors shutting

on dreams too slow to run.

The noise never ends—

it just shifts,

silence and sound in a slow, sick dance.

A fever that can't break.

It never does.

A woman walks by,

her shoes slapping the wet pavement

like the sound of defeat.

She's got a stroller full of nothing—

a baby's cries muffled by the clang of metal,

the screech of tires,

the thousand lives spinning out of control.

Her eyes are lost,

like a ship that's been out to sea too long,

searching for a shore that never comes.

She keeps moving—

because what else is there to do?

What else is there

but keep moving,

even when the city is eating you alive?

The junkie in the alley doesn't move anymore.

He's staring at the needle like it's his last lover,

and the high's the only thing

that ever made him feel something—

anything—

other than empty.

You can see it in his eyes—

the hunger to escape,

the hunger to be more than this—

but there's no running from this city.

No matter how far you go.

It doesn't let you go.

It just wears you down.

The bar on the corner?

That neon flickers like a broken heart,

the red glow a promise that's always betrayed.

Inside, the drunks drink away their ghosts,

but they drown in their own spit and sweat,

gasping for air that smells like failure.

Somewhere in the back,

a poet scribbles on a napkin,

writing the last lines of a life he never wanted,

but never had the courage to leave behind.

His hand shakes—

but the words don't come.

The city's louder than the page.

The city's always louder.

This city doesn't care about you.

It'll chew you up and spit you out,

give you just enough to keep you hungry,

just enough to keep you moving.

The rich walk by,

eyes straight ahead,

too scared to look down

at the mess they're making.

Too scared to see the world breaking

beneath their feet.

You think they've got it made?

You think they've found the answer?

They're the real beggars here.

They wear suits instead of rags,

they hide their hunger with a smile,

but they're dying too.

They're just dying slower.

But us?

We know something they don't.

We're still here—

still breathing,

still creating,

still fighting to make something beautiful

in the wreckage.

We've got nothing left to lose—

so we're free in ways they'll never be.

# HOMELESS IN NEW YORK

The graffiti on the wall says it all:

"We're still fucking here."

And it doesn't matter if they paint over it—

because it's burned into the bones of this place.

It's permanent.

It'll never go away.

Not as long as we're still fucking here.

The poets, the artists, the thieves, the broken—

we're all the same,

scraping our names into the dirt,

hoping someone will see us,

even if we don't exist in their world.

We keep moving,

because what else is there to do?

What else is there to say?

We create—

because creation is the last thing

this city hasn't stolen from us.

We paint on the mess,

we write in the blood,

and we keep going—

because even this,

even this fucked-up city,

can't take that away from us.

It doesn't get to steal our fire.

Not today.

Not ever.

Maybe that's the only art that matters—

fighting back against the city,

fighting back against the hunger,

fighting back against the idea

that you can ever truly be broken.

You're not broken.

You're just bent.

And bent still makes a shape.

A broken thing can still create.

The shattered glass cuts deep—

but those pieces

reflect the light.

---

YOU THINK I'M INVISIBLE, don't you? You see the rags, the tired eyes, the dirt beneath my fingernails, and you pretend I'm not here. You walk by like I'm a stain on the sidewalk, a mistake you can't wash off fast enough. But I'm here. I've always been here. The streets know me, and I know them. The concrete's like an old lover, cruel and cold, but it's mine. You can't feel the weight of it the way I do. Your shiny shoes can dance around it, but I have to drag my soul through it every fucking day.

I don't need your kindness, your spare change. I'm not some sad story for your conscience. I'm not your charity project. I've got a mind, a pulse, a fire inside that burns hotter than the nicest house in the city. You think the city belongs to the rich? That they're the only ones who matter? They just got lucky. They don't know what it means to survive—really survive. You think you've got it figured out? You think a suit and a smile buys you happiness? Bullshit. You're just running from your own emptiness. At least I'm honest about mine.

You're scared to look down at me, at the other lost souls rotting in this concrete jungle. But you can't look away forever. You can't erase what you don't see. We're here. We're loud. The world tries to bury us under its pretty lies, but you'll hear us screaming under your perfect silence.

Maybe that's what you're scared of—that the city won't let you forget. That even if you paint over our words, the truth is still burned into the walls. We're still here. Still fucking here.

# A Roofless Cathedral

Finding shelter in a street corner, and the church of people who struggle together.

WE SLEEP UNDER A SKY

that doesn't even blink.

Stars don't look down—they spit,

flicker out like old sparks

in the gutters of this city

that loves the rich and ignores the rest.

The rats are the real royalty here,

the junkies, the saints.

Gold runs through their veins,

their prayers swallowed in syringes,

inhaling the city's poison

like a mother's kiss—

but it's all just survival,

all just another way to stay alive

when you're already dead inside.

We don't need roofs,

not when we've got each other,

not when this corner is our cathedral,

the sidewalk our altar.

The shadows don't judge,

they take us in,

wrap us up in their cold embrace,

and the wind?

It's sharp as a knife

cutting through our bones,

but we've learned to love it.

The preacher with his cardboard sign

keeps talking salvation,

like there's a coupon for it,

like you can buy it cheap

on the street corner.

But we know better—

this city doesn't give a damn

about salvation,

it only wants to know

if you're strong enough to survive.

You survive here

or you disappear.

The streets are littered with ghosts,

people who were too weak,

too tired, too broken

to stay in the fight.

But we fight.

We fight with our eyes open,

with our hands out,

digging through the trash

for scraps of dignity,

for a moment's peace.

They call us forgotten,

insignificant,

but who are they to say?

They don't know the taste of survival,

the sweet, sour taste of living

when you're already dead inside.

They think they can look through us,

but we see them.

We see the lies

they sell from their glass towers,

the lives they forget with every step,

the city they built on our backs

while pretending we don't exist.

We don't need their mercy.

We don't need their pity.

We don't need anything but each other.

In this broken place,

we've built something holy—

a roofless cathedral

where the only god is the will

to keep breathing,

to keep moving,

to keep going,

even when the ground is nothing

but jagged glass and spilled blood.

We made this place ours

with nothing but hunger and rage.

They don't see it,

but we've built it from the wreckage—

the sanctuary in the trash,

the redemption in the cracks,

and no one,

no one

can take it from us.

We don't need their salvation.

We don't need their church,

or their books,

or their prayers.

We have our own rites,

our own ways of knowing

that we're alive

even when we're invisible.

And that's the only truth that matters—

we're still here.

We're still here,

and we'll keep breathing,

keep surviving,

even as they turn their eyes away

and pretend we're not.

The city has forgotten us,

but we haven't forgotten each other.

We built this church with our hands—

cracked, bleeding,

covered in the dirt

they think they can erase.

And it's ours.

All ours.

We're not invisible.

We're the city's backbone,

the ones who hold it up,

who keep it running,

while they make their fortunes,

climbing higher,

trampling us beneath their feet.

But we survive.

We survive because we know

that survival is the only thing left

worth fighting for.

And in the end,

maybe that's the only goddamn miracle

that's left.

---

I DON'T WANT YOUR SYMPATHY. Don't look at me like I'm some broken thing you can fix with a couple of coins or a kind word that's as empty as your promises. I'm not a charity case or a tragic story to share over dinner. You think you know me because you see me on the corner, wrapped in a filthy blanket, fingers raw from the cold. You don't. You don't know the first thing about what it's like to wake up to nothing but concrete, the sound of traffic in your ears and your own hunger gnawing at you like a dog that's been fed nothing but scraps for weeks.

This place—this corner—is the only cathedral I've got. I built it with my hands. My bones. My sweat. My blood. And don't you dare tell me it's not holy, that it's not sacred. It's more real than the garbage they call "life" up there in their glass towers, where they think success is a number on a paycheck and happiness is a vacation in the Bahamas. Here, we survive. We don't pray to your god, we don't need your bullshit salvation. We've got each other and that's more than enough. You think we're forgotten? That we're invisible? Well, maybe to you. But we see everything. We see how you walk by, heads down, eyes glazed over like you can't even be bothered to glance at us. You build your empire on our backs, then tell us we're the problem.

Yeah, we fight. And we win. Not because we've got the luxury of a roof over our heads, but because we're alive, and that's the hardest thing in this world to be. We're not asking for your mercy. We don't need it. We've got this—this roofless cathedral where survival's the only damn god worth worshipping.

# 42nd Street Part 1 - The Corner of 42nd Street

The intersection of humanity and despair in one of the busiest and most
bustling parts of New York.

*A ROOFLESS CATHEDRAL*

1.

The city hums like a wound stitched with wires

and glass—42nd Street,

the pulse of ambition,

and here, beneath the towering gods

of marble and chrome,

I am a stain that won't scrub away.

A patch of dirt you'd step over

if you weren't in a rush to get to somewhere

where everything sparkles,

where money can buy dignity

and the homeless are just statistics

on some bleeding chart.

I stretch my arms out to the sky,

but it's a roofless cathedral,

no pews,

no priests with silver tongues.

Just the sound of your footsteps,

the ones that won't slow down,

the ones that look at the ground

so you don't see me,

so you don't see your reflection

in my cracked skin.

The rats own the subway grates,

the pigeons wear the city like a crown.

There's a wisdom in their bones

you never learned

with your shiny briefcase and your tie,

but I'm the one who knows the secret:

the world is already falling apart

before you rebuild it again.

Your cathedral doesn't save you,

it just numbs the blood

until it gets so thick

you can't hear the screams.

I'm the prayers you won't say,

the hope you forgot how to feel.

**HOMELESS IN NEW YORK**

You'll walk past me again,

in a city where nothing ever stops moving,

not even the silence in my chest.

But I'm still here,

still breathing the stink of this sidewalk,

still holding onto this cracked crown

of cardboard and whiskey.

I don't need your pity.

I don't need your half-hearted promises.

I'm a witness to your city,

and it's got nothing left to give.

You know it,

I know it.

And we're both pretending

that you'll ever fix what's broken

or find a place where your hands

won't be trembling from the weight

of everything you've forgotten to care about.

---

*42ND STREET PART 2 - Times Square*

2.

**ALEX TELMAN**

THE LIGHTS IN TIMES Square are electric veins,

pulsing in sync with a city that swallows its own,

chews up the broken and spits them out—

pieces of skin,

pieces of life,

pieces of a man

who used to think he could have it all.

Under the digital glow,

I sit, a black-and-white film

on the edge of color.

They rush by,

grinning into their screens,

slaves to a future that promised them

what they already gave away.

In the city of neon gods,

I am invisible—

a ghost in the land of living dreams,

haunted by the taste of things I'll never touch.

The billboards scream,

freedom!

fame!

happiness!

104

but they're just plastic promises

wrapped in shiny paper.

I've seen their faces.

I've heard their lies.

The city hums its song—

a tune that once made me dance,

but now it grinds against my bones.

The tourists glance,

see me for a second,

then look away.

A pause.

A hesitation.

Then they're gone,

off to buy their happiness

in the form of souvenirs and lies.

I am not part of their picture.

I don't fit in their frame.

The lights—they burn,

but they never warm.

They glow with all the intensity

of a world that refuses to notice

its own collapse.

They dance to a rhythm I can't follow—

too fast,

too bright,

too fleeting.

I want to scream—

but my voice is swallowed by the noise

of a city that never stops

talking.

I want to ask them if they hear it,

the scream of the street,

the silence of the forgotten,

but I know better.

They wouldn't understand.

They don't even see me.

The taxis honk their horns

like angry gods,

as the crowds spill into the street,

shoving past each other

on their way to nowhere.

In the blur of flesh and glass,

I am a shadow—

melted into the asphalt,

# HOMELESS IN NEW YORK

just another part of the city

no one cares to notice.

The sirens scream a song I know well,

familiar as the ache in my chest.

They scream,

but nothing changes.

The sound fades—

and the city keeps spinning,

keeps moving,

keeps living as if we're all

in this together.

But I am not in this.

I am not part of the city's heartbeat.

I am the one who stands still,

watching them race by,

wondering how they don't see the cracks

in the concrete,

the hollowed-out faces in the crowd,

the ones who can't keep up.

The lights flicker,

but they will not save me.

They will not save any of us.

Not as long as the price of living

keeps rising,

and the cost of surviving

keeps sinking.

This city is a graveyard of dreams.

A thousand glittering graves,

a thousand vacant eyes.

I sit in the middle of it,

waiting for something to give—

waiting for a moment

when the neon will stop flashing

long enough to see me.

But it never happens.

The city dances to its own song.

I am not invited to the party.

And I never will be.

I'm just a forgotten verse

in the back of the music,

too far away to ever make it to the front.

But that's fine.

That's real.

The lights can keep shining—

they won't burn me anymore.

And I won't burn for them.

I'll stay here,

on the edge of everything,

watching their parade pass by.

Because somewhere in the darkness,

I am alive.

And maybe that's enough.

---

YOU WALK BY ME, DON'T you? You walk by like I'm not here. Like I'm some piece of trash you can't even be bothered to step over. The neon lights blink at you, flashing promises that are as hollow as the concrete I sleep on. You think you know the city, right? You think you understand it. You think you're alive in it, don't you? But you're not. Not really. You're all just ghosts, walking in the shadow of a machine that doesn't care about you any more than it cares about me. Maybe even less. You buy your tickets to the show, ride the Ferris wheel of empty promises, and I'm left here, the same as I've always been. A face you won't look at twice. A voice you won't hear.

But I hear you. I hear your hollow chatter, your desperate, empty talk about dreams that have already been sold to you at a price you didn't even ask for. You tell me to pick myself up, to stop dragging myself around in this gutter of a city. You tell me I could have more, but you don't know what it's like to bleed for it. You don't know what it's like to crawl through the dirt with nothing but your teeth to bite down on. You don't know what it means to be invisible in a city that eats people for breakfast, spits out their bones for lunch, and forgets their names by dinner.

I watch the lights flash in Times Square like they've got something to show me. Like they've got something to offer. The billboards scream about freedom, happiness, success. All of it lit up in dazzling colors. But you and I both know it's just the shine of a rotting carcass. The city's pulse is loud, but it doesn't make me feel alive. The sirens scream, and the taxis honk, but it's just noise. None of it is real. There's no truth in the flashing lights, no warmth in the glow. Just a cold, heartless city beating a rhythm that no one can follow.

And the people. Oh, the people. They rush by, heads bent down, eyes locked to their screens like they're afraid to look at what's really here, afraid to face the truth. The truth that they're all just as lost as me, just wearing better clothes and living in nicer boxes. You're all chasing something that you'll never catch, pushing and shoving your way through the streets like there's a prize waiting for you at the end. But when you get there, you'll be just like me. Alone. You'll find your dream, your shiny, polished dream, and you'll look at it, and you'll know it's not what you thought it would be. You'll look at it, and all you'll see is a reflection of how empty you are inside.

So go ahead. Keep your lights. Keep your crowds. Keep your noise. It doesn't matter. You can buy whatever you want, but you'll never buy the one thing that means anything in this city—realness. The truth of this place is written in the cracks of the pavement, in the faded neon lights, in the garbage that's left behind after the crowds have gone. It's there in the faces you won't look at, in the ones you can't see because you've got your blinders on.

But I see it. I see it all. I've got no choice but to. I watch the world pass me by, and I know what I am in this city. I'm not a part of it. I'm not a cog in the machine. I'm not a pretty picture in your frame. I'm the dirt under your feet. I'm the stain you can't wash out. I'm the thing you ignore until it's too late. And maybe that's alright. Because I'm still here, aren't I? Still breathing. Still surviving. While you chase your dreams, I'm still watching from the gutter, and maybe that's the only truth that matters.

# The Homeless Have Stories, Too

A look at the individual lives, stories, and dreams of the people who are often forgotten.

1.

They sleep on streets that spit at the sky,

their faces cracked by cold and sun,

like old leather wallets discarded in the gutter.

The ones with nothing but their bones,

their hands blackened by the years

they spent chasing dreams that dissolved

like steam from the subway grates.

You walk past them, don't even blink,

but they're there,

always there,

like shadows that refuse to die.

The ones who never made it out

of the corner they were born in,

the ones whose names you'll never know,

whose lives mean less than the crumbs

beneath the foot of some tourist

clutching a plastic cup of overpriced coffee.

They sit on the pavement,

hunched over like broken statues,

eyes filled with the ghosts of yesterday,

their stories fading in the noise

of the city's electric heart.

Some of them once wore suits,

held meetings in glass towers,

drove cars with polished chrome,

but that was before the fall,

before the city chewed them up

and spit them out,

its promises broken,

like the sidewalk cracks they sleep beside.

They wake up to the hum of traffic,

the buzz of neon lights that flicker

as they vanish into the void

of someone else's life.

You've heard the rumors—

they're lazy, they're addicted,

they're the refuse of society,

but have you ever asked them

about the stories they carry?

The ones that didn't make it into the headlines,

the ones that got lost in the cracks of glass

and cigarette smoke?

Maybe one of them dreamed

of being a doctor, a lawyer,

someone who saved lives.

Maybe another was a soldier,

fighting in wars that no one remembers,

and now the only battle they fight

is for a corner of concrete

that's theirs for the night.

They're not just bodies scattered like garbage,

they're the forgotten,

the invisible,

the ones who used to matter

before they didn't.

Each one has a name,

a story you'll never hear,

a life that could've been,

but wasn't.

They have the same scars

you hide with your coat and tie,

the same hunger

that gnaws at your bones

when the world doesn't care,

the same empty spaces

where dreams used to be.

But you won't look at them,

won't ask,

because if you did,

you might see yourself.

———————————————

2.

They don't get it, do they?

They walk by with their shiny shoes,

their latte cups raised high like trophies

they've earned for doing something noble,

and they never look down.

Down where the real stories are.

Where the bones are sharp against the skin,

where the days blur into one endless blur

of hunger and longing for just a minute of warmth.

# HOMELESS IN NEW YORK

You think you've made it, don't you?

Made it out of the gutter, out of the mess

you were born into,

but you're one bad decision,

one unlucky break from landing right back here.

Here, where we learn the real names of things.

Not the names of the rich or the famous—

those are like whispers in the wind.

Here, we know the names of the streets,

the names of the benches,

the names of the gutters and the cracks in the sidewalk

that catch the rain and turn it to mud.

You think we're lazy?

That we're addicts?

You think we're all just drifting,

waiting for some handout,

waiting for someone to lift us

from this concrete coffin?

You don't know a goddamn thing.

You don't know the battles,

the wars we've fought in our heads,

the ones where we've lost over and over again

but still got up to fight tomorrow.

You don't know what it's like to watch

your life unravel

like a cheap sweater,

to stand in line for food

while they treat you like you're invisible,

like you're less than human,

like you're the dirt beneath their shoes.

You don't know how it feels

to have every dream you ever had

slip through your fingers

like sand that gets washed away in a storm.

You can't know what it's like

to have the world turn its back on you,

because you're too busy

climbing your little tower of success,

pretending like you've got it all figured out.

We're not here because we want to be.

We're here because we've been forgotten,

because the world's got no room for people

who don't fit its clean little boxes.

But we still have stories.

You want to know about them?

You want to know how we got here?

We'll tell you.

But you'll never understand,

because you don't want to.

You don't want to see us for what we are—

people,

just like you,

only we've learned the hard way

that nothing in this world is guaranteed,

not love, not loyalty,

not the hope that someday you'll be someone else.

We're the leftovers.

The ones who fell through the cracks.

But don't think for a second

that we don't have stories worth telling.

We're not invisible.

We're just ignored.

3.

It's funny, isn't it? The way they look at us, like we're something less.

You can smell the disgust in their eyes.

They think we don't see it, but we do. We always do.

They cross the street or look away,

as if we're nothing but a stain on their perfect world.

They've never been where we are—

never stood on this corner in the dead of night,

hands shoved deep in your pockets,

waiting for the next hit of warmth from a passing car

or the faintest promise that tomorrow will be different.

They think we're all junkies or drunks,

too lazy or too broken to climb out of our own shit.

They don't know what it's like to watch the world slip away

like a cracked sidewalk under your feet,

a lifetime of missed chances, bad choices,

and things you can't undo.

They don't know the sound of a dumpster lid

slamming down on your last meal,

the way the cold bites through your skin

like it's got a personal vendetta against you.

They don't want to know, though.

Why would they?

We're just the forgotten ones,

the invisible ones,

the ones who get tossed aside when we stop being useful.

# HOMELESS IN NEW YORK

But here's the thing:

We still have stories.

We're not just faces in the dirt.

We've been through things,

things they could never imagine.

And maybe we're fucked up,

maybe we're lost,

but we're not dead.

Not yet.

Not until they bury us under the next shiny building

or step over us without a second thought.

So yeah,

we've got stories.

You think we don't?

You think we don't have something to say?

Well, listen up,

because when the world forgets you,

you don't forget yourself.

You just learn how to survive.

And that, my friend, is a story worth telling.

Waking Up in the Rain

- The physical realities of homelessness, such as being drenched in rain with no shelter.

---

THE SKY'S A FIST,

its knuckles split open with clouds,

and I wake cold,

drenched in the gutter,

where the pavement smells of piss and rot,

where rats march like soldiers,

in a war that never ends.

The city doesn't care.

It churns its iron heart,

beats with the pulse of glass and steel,

and I'm just a stain on the sidewalk,

a ripple in the gutter,

too small to be seen,

too soaked to be saved.

A man with a briefcase steps over me,

his shoes too clean for these streets,

his eyes too focused on the future

to bother with what's rotting in the present.

# HOMELESS IN NEW YORK

He doesn't see me—

but that's not the worst part.

The worst part is that

I don't see him either.

The rain's a hammer,

pounding me into the earth,

pounding the world into shape,

but it never shapes anything,

just leaves the cracks

where they've always been—

a patchwork of broken lives,

forgotten souls,

lost things.

The sound of the rain is like a prayer,

but there's no God to answer it—

just the hiss of tires on wet pavement,

the wail of sirens,

like the city trying to mourn

its own ugly reflection,

but too busy to know how.

So it keeps moving,

keeps grinding,

as if it's too deaf

to hear what it's killing.

I saw a drunk this morning,

his hand shaking as he tried to light a cigarette—

the match flared,

then died in the rain,

like his dreams.

He doesn't notice.

He's too far gone,

shoulders heavy with a weight

he doesn't even feel.

The rain falls like a curse,

but he's already cursed,

waiting to be buried in it.

Across the street,

a woman with red lips,

redder than the blood that never spills

on the sidewalks she walks,

steps past,

heels clicking like a countdown

to a death she won't see coming,

a death she'll never notice.

# HOMELESS IN NEW YORK

She thinks the rain won't touch her,

but it will—

it touches everyone,

sooner or later.

A child looks at me

like I'm something to be feared,

her innocence still bright,

still unbroken,

but it won't stay that way.

She'll grow up to be like the rest of us—

sheltered in a world

that doesn't care who gets left behind.

She'll learn that people

aren't born into the rain.

We're made by it.

We are the rain.

I want to scream,

but what's the point?

The noise of the city is deafening,

drowning out the voice of anyone

who isn't already part of the machine,

the machine that hums on,

no matter how many of us get crushed in the gears.

The rain doesn't stop.

It never does.

It's not here to cleanse,

not here to wash anything away—

it's here to remind us

that we are all just water,

washing over the cracks in the city,

filling them up,

only to spill over

and leave them empty again.

I saw a man with a dog

this morning—

the dog's eyes are older than mine,

too tired to bark,

too tired to run,

but the man pats its head,

thinking that the touch

might heal something—

but it won't.

Nothing will.

Not for him.

# HOMELESS IN NEW YORK

Not for me.

Not for anyone.

The woman in red,

the businessman,

the kid—they'll all keep walking,

blind to the ruin they leave behind.

And the rain will keep falling,

a cold reminder

that we're all just passing through,

waiting for something

that never comes.

I close my eyes

and listen to the rhythm of the world,

to the thrum of tires on wet roads,

the hiss of rain on rooftops,

the muffled footfalls of the invisible,

the forgotten,

the ones who'll never be remembered.

I hear it all,

and it doesn't matter.

Tomorrow,

I'll wake up here again,

cold,

wet,

and waiting for a world that will never come for me.

But I'll be here,

in the rain,

waiting for the next thing to pass me by,

waiting for the next death,

waiting for the next breath

that never quite reaches my lungs.

I am what the city doesn't want to see,

what it spits on,

what it leaves in the gutter—

but I am also what it can never wash away.

I am the forgotten thing

that lives in the rain.

---

THE CITY DOESN'T GIVE a damn about me. That's the truth of it. I'm just another body on the pavement, one more shadow the sun will never warm. The rain? It's not here to wash me clean, it's here to remind me of my place. The same gutter I wake up in every day, soaked through, skin tight with cold, bones gnawing at me like they're hungry for something I can't give.

People walk by, thinking they don't see me. But they don't realize they're just as invisible as I am. They've got their shiny shoes and their plastic dreams, pretending they've got something to live for. But the truth is, they're dying in slow motion too, just like the rest of us. They just don't see it yet. Hell, they probably won't until they're lying in some shitty hospital bed, waiting for death to make up its mind.

The rain falls, cold as hell, beating down like it's got a purpose. But it doesn't. It's not here to save me or anyone else. It's here to drown out the noise, to make the world feel a little quieter, a little emptier. There's no god up there, no higher plan. Just water and cement and broken hearts, nothing more.

I've got no illusions. I don't wake up hoping for a handout. I don't care if anyone notices me. People have got their own problems. They're too busy dying inside to stop and look at someone who's already gone. So I stay here, in the rain, in the dirt, where the world won't touch me. Where it can't touch me. Where it can't take anything more from me. I'm already as empty as this godforsaken street. And I'll stay that way, until the next damn rain comes.

# The Cold Concrete Pillow

A poem about the loneliness of sleeping on hard surfaces and the comfort found in simple acts.

I LIE ON THE GROUND like a dog

that's forgotten the sound of its own bark.

The concrete—stone cut from a dead world,

carved by hands that didn't care

if it crushed or cradled.

It doesn't care if I sleep or wake,

if I breathe or die.

It just lies there,

cold as the soul of this city,

cold as the hand that shakes you awake

in a dream you can't recall.

People walk over me,

rushing, stepping light on their heavy shoes,

too busy to notice

the clocks ticking under their feet,

the ones that'll never tell time right again.

I watch their shadows stretch,

slip through cracks,

like ghosts with no home,

no name,

no reason to stay.

I can feel them,

but I'm too far gone

to ask where they're headed

or if they'll look back.

The cold concrete pillow doesn't care

how tired my body gets,

how fractured my mind is

from wars it can't win.

I curl like a thing already dead,

pressing my skin into its jagged back,

waiting for the night to stretch out,

to swallow me whole,

to erase me.

I've learned how to sleep like this—

not in pieces,

but in splinters,

half a mind still watching,

half a body still aching,

half a heart still hoping

for something that won't come.

But when the first light hits the pavement—

that soft gold spill of nothing,

it touches the edges of my eyes,

and for one second,

I feel it—

a touch,

a breath of warmth

that makes me think maybe

I'm not as lost as I feel.

The cigarette burns at the corner of my mouth—

I suck on it like it's the last breath I'll ever get,

but the city won't care.

It snuffs out flames quicker than love,

quicker than hope,

quicker than dreams—

it buries them in the cracks of the street,

where no one will bother to look.

I glance up at the sky,

dirty with the breath of a thousand forgotten promises,

too many clouds to count,

too tired to cry.

The stars?

Haven't seen them in years.

They're up there somewhere,

lost behind the smog of ambition,

buried beneath the weight of lives

lived for nothing,

for lives too small to matter.

But it doesn't matter—

the sky's the same,

even if it never looks the way it's supposed to.

I roll over,

press my cheek to the concrete

like a lover whose touch is too cold

but whose body still knows how to hold.

The street's a stranger,

but it's the only one I've got—

the only one that doesn't ask for answers,

doesn't ask if I'm coming or going.

It just lets me be,

like the rest of the things

the city doesn't see.

And that's the only kind of comfort

I'll ever know.

When I wake,

there's the hum of traffic,

the grinding pulse of the city—

it never stops for anyone,

not for the homeless,

not for the desperate,

not for the ones who sleep on cold concrete pillows

with no one to call them home.

I get up,

brush the dirt off my clothes

like it's the only thing I still own.

I'll make my way through the streets again,

dodging eyes,

slipping between the cracks,

just another face the city never bothers to look at.

But I don't mind.

It's the only thing I can count on—

being invisible in a world

too loud to hear

what's dying in the silence.

And when the night falls again,

I'll lay back down

on my cold concrete pillow,

and the city will keep moving,

and I'll keep waiting

for something that will never come.

But that's alright.

I've got nowhere else to be.

––––––––––––

THEY DON'T KNOW. THEY never will. They walk around with their clean shoes, their shiny bags, their tight little smiles, and they think they're free. They think they're alive, but they're all just ghosts. 'I' know what it feels like to have nothing. Nothing but the cold concrete under your back, the wind biting at your bones like a hungry dog. You think it's cruel? It's more than that—it's indifferent. The concrete doesn't care about me. It doesn't care about anyone. People call it hard, but I call it honest. The street doesn't lie to you. It doesn't whisper promises it can't keep. It's brutal, but it's true. If you're alive, it'll let you know. If you're dead, it'll let you rot.

I've learned how to sleep on it—on this cold slab, on this stone that has no memory of yesterday or tomorrow. It's a place for the forgotten. A place where the ghosts of dreams lie down to die. And every night, I lie down with them. You get used to it. There's a rhythm to it. People rush over you, walk past you, act like they can't see you, like you're a shadow they can ignore. Maybe they think I don't hear the way their steps get quicker when they're close. Maybe they think I don't feel the heat from their bodies as they speed by, the heat that doesn't reach me. Maybe they think I don't notice the way they cross the street, avoiding my stare like it's some kind of plague.

But you can't avoid it forever.

You think I'm a 'failure'? You think I've lost the game? Well, hell, maybe I have, but I'm still here, aren't I? And this concrete pillow—this cold, unforgiving slab—it's as much of a companion as anyone has ever been. At least it's honest. At least it's not pretending to be something it's not. It doesn't try to sell you shit. It doesn't tell you that tomorrow's gonna be better or that you're worth something. It just is.

The world will tell you you're invisible. They'll tell you you're a ghost. But it's them who can't see. They can't see how real it is when the cold bites through your skin and the night wraps itself around your bones like it's the only blanket you'll ever have. They can't feel what it's like to be seen and still be nothing.

But I've learned something. The stars are out there, too—hidden behind the city's smog, buried under ambition and greed. Maybe I can't touch them, but they're still up there, aren't they? Still burning. Still out there, in the vastness. Just like me.

**23. Chasing Warmth in a Diner** (Revised)

- The small acts of kindness in public spaces, and the struggle to find comfort in the cold.

---

THE BELL ABOVE THE door rings

like the sound of someone giving up,

but you're already inside,

already caught in the soft hum of the diner's belly,

a man with nowhere to go,

nowhere to be but here,

between the bitter pull of smoke

and the last drag of a world that's too tired

to notice you.

The place smells like regret

and grease fried so many times

it could forget its own name.

The waitress's eyes are vacant,

and she slides a menu in front of you,

like it's a script you've already learned.

You won't need it.

You need heat.

You need something to fill that hollow space

where the cold has claimed the bones,

stole the warmth like a thief at dawn.

Her fingers brush yours when she sets down

the coffee, too hot,

like it could burn away everything,

but you drink it slow,

because the warmth comes at a price—

it always does.

For a second, the skin on your lips remembers

what it was like to feel like you belong

to the world, not just a stranger passing through.

The heat settles like a promise,

but you know it's a lie.

Just a few minutes,

just enough to remind you

that for some, comfort is always fleeting,

like a joke you never quite catch.

Outside, the wind slices through the streets

like the last breath of something forgotten.

It rips open the edges of the city,

fraying the lives stitched together

by hands that can't stop trembling.

# HOMELESS IN NEW YORK

The world outside presses in,

too fast, too cold,

as if it knows your name,

but never cares to speak it.

The waitress moves past,

her eyes glazed,

lost in a loop of motions she's forgotten

have meaning.

You don't know her,

but for a second,

you think she might know something about

what it means to disappear—

to be the person everyone steps over

on their way to somewhere.

The old man by the window doesn't see you,

but he feels the same cold you do.

The two men arguing over baseball

like they have a future to argue about,

their voices louder than the rest of the world,

drowning out the quietest truths:

you'll never be a part of this.

And the woman stirring sugar into her tea,

the spoon turning the liquid like a clock

that's stopped ticking.

They're all lost,

and so are you.

But for now, you're warm.

Not full,

not alive in any real way,

but warm.

And sometimes that's all you can ask for—

a few seconds of heat in a world

that doesn't even notice your name.

You slide the mug back across the counter,

leaving coins like a tip for a debt you'll never repay.

She takes them with the same motion

she's used a thousand times,

and the nod she gives you is empty

but somehow still full of meaning—

like a lie that feels true,

like warmth that feels like it might last

but always slips away.

Outside, the wind howls

like it knows you're still here,

but the cold doesn't matter anymore,

because you're breathing.

Just enough to remember

that you haven't disappeared yet.

The world doesn't care,

but you're still here,

still waiting for the next warmth,

the next lie,

the next second where you'll feel

like you're not invisible

and the cold is someone else's problem.

---

YOU THINK ANYONE GIVES a damn about the guy shivering in the corner booth? You think they see me? Nah. I'm invisible, man. I've got the kind of invisibility you don't just get. You earn it after years of being the wrong kind of human. The kind that sits in diners with stained cups and broken coats, begging for warmth like it's something we're supposed to get, like a promise we're entitled to.

I chase it. That warmth. Like some junkie chasing a hit, never quite sure if I'll catch it or not. But when it hits, man, you'd swear it could fix everything. I sip that coffee like it's something that could save me. One sip and suddenly I'm somebody. Maybe somebody who's not dying in the street, maybe somebody who's alive, even if it's just for a minute. But you know better. It never lasts. It never does. Like the steam fogging up the window, all that heat and comfort disappears just as fast as it came, leaving nothing but a bitter aftertaste.

The waitress thinks I'm just another one of the deadbeats who'll slide in, order something he can't afford, and leave without a word. But she doesn't know what I'm doing. I'm not just waiting for my meal. I'm waiting for my soul to feel like it's more than a pile of bones and bad choices. You try living like this and not want to steal a second of comfort. One second where you're not just some walking body. One second where you're not some loser, some forgotten fuck-up.

And the world? It keeps moving. It keeps passing by. The other people in the diner—they don't see me. They don't see anything but their own lives, their own little problems that matter more than mine. They're too busy arguing over some dumb baseball game to notice the man with the ragged coat sitting by the window, freezing his ass off. They'll keep talking, like they've got time. Like time isn't just slipping away from us both. Like they'll never know what it feels like to have nowhere to go, nowhere to be. No one to give a shit about them.

Yeah, that warmth—it's a joke. But I'll take it, every damn time. It's the only thing that reminds me I'm still here. I'm not dead yet. And that's worth something.

100

# Invisible from the Upper East Side

A reflection on the class divide between the wealthy and the dispossessed in one of the city's richest neighbourhoods.

1.

I'M NOT HERE.

Not in their world.

I slip between cracks—

beneath their shiny shoes,

the ones that never touch the concrete,

the ones that float above it all,

while I crawl with the rats

through piss and the smell of last night's drunk.

They think I'm a ghost.

I'm not—

I'm just not visible.

They walk by like I'm part of the scenery—

like I'm another broken sidewalk,

just another stain in the corner of their view.

## HOMELESS IN NEW YORK

But I'm real,

and I'm fucking tired of being invisible.

They live in the air,

I live in the ground.

Their towers are made of glass,

their lives of illusion,

and all of it's held up by my back,

the backs of the forgotten,

the ones they pretend not to see.

But they feel it.

They always feel it.

The ache that comes when the truth

starts breaking through their shiny shoes.

But they look away.

If they saw me,

they'd have to see themselves.

And they can't afford that.

They'd rather keep the blindfold on,

pretend they aren't standing in the dirt

that was never meant for them.

A hundred bucks for coffee—

does it taste like privilege?

Does it taste like death?

The way it sits in their gut

and makes them forget

how it feels to wake up with the cold

knowing no one's coming to help.

But they never feel it,

because their skin is covered

in fabric that says "I don't care."

They wear their masks

and act like they're untouchable.

Like their blood doesn't boil,

like they don't know

their hearts beat the same as mine.

But they think they're better.

Better because they've got a job

and a coat that costs a month's rent.

Better because they buy happiness

with their wallets

and can walk away from the rest of us

like we're a forgotten street sign.

I'm not invisible.

I'm just the mirror.

# HOMELESS IN NEW YORK

They can't look at me

without seeing their reflection

crack.

But I'm not the one

who's broken.

I'm the one who still exists

after they've walked by.

And when their towers come down,

I'll still be here.

I'll be here when their mirrors shatter,

and maybe then,

they'll see what I've been trying to say

this whole time.

———————

2.

———————

LOOK AT ME.

I'm not some sorry excuse for a man to be swept into the cracks of your conscience,

no, I'm the reflection you're too scared to look at.

I don't need your handouts.

I don't need your faux charity that comes with a smile

and a mental pat on the back like you've done something special.

I'm not your pet project.

I'm the wreckage of a system built on the backs of people like me.

But you, you stroll by in your suits,

your shiny shoes tapping on the pavement like you own it,

like the world was made to cradle you,

like the air was specially filtered for your breath.

You've never tasted the cold of a sidewalk,

never felt the bite of wind cutting through your coat,

the kind that makes your bones ache

and your soul feel like it might just slip through your ribs

and leave you hollow inside.

You don't know what it's like to have to fight for every inch of warmth.

You think a $5 bill in your hand is an answer to everything.

But it's not.

You toss it at me like I'm some kind of beggar,

a charity case,

but I'm not.

I'm a mirror you don't want to see,

a truth that you'd rather step over than face.

I don't need your clean streets and polished corners,

your fancy cafes where you sip on your overpriced lattes

and talk about your latest self-help book.

What are you helping?

Yourself?

Because if you're helping anyone,

it's not people like me.

You hide your faces behind tinted windows,

your lives are lived in bubbles,

bubbles that pop when you touch anything that smells like struggle.

You don't see me.

You never see me.

But I'm here.

I've always been here.

I'll be here when your towers of glass and steel fall.

I'll be here long after your fortunes vanish in the blink of an eye.

I've got nothing left to lose,

and that's the thing you'll never understand—

how free that can make you.

Because I'm the part of you that you don't want to know,

the part you think you can ignore.

But I'm the truth you can't outrun.

You can build your towers,

you can dress yourself in a thousand-dollar coat,

but I'm the one who'll still be standing

when the storm hits.

And you'll see me then.

You'll see me when the polished world turns to dust.

———————————

3.

———————————

YOU DON'T SEE ME, DO you? You walk right past, eyes glazed over,

your fancy shoes clicking on the sidewalk like you're walking on air.

Your leather bags, your perfect lives—you can taste it, can't you?

The comfort, the warmth, the safety of your little world.

But me? I'm just a shadow in your reflection. I'm invisible.

You don't want to know what it's like to be me.

To be here, on the edge, where the city spits you out like you never mattered.

Where the cold seeps into your bones and nobody notices.

Nobody cares.

You think I'm just a statistic,

a face with a cardboard sign, a rattle in my cup—

but you don't even look at me long enough to see my eyes.

They're the same eyes you've got.

You think I'm a charity case,

someone to toss a dollar at when you feel guilty

or maybe when you've had one too many drinks

and your conscience goes soft for a second.

But I'm not your charity case. I'm the truth.

I'm the unspoken word you keep tucked away in the back of your head,

the one that says maybe you're not as untouchable as you think.

I'm the crack in your shiny, perfect world

that you pretend doesn't exist

but I'm here, right here,

just as real as the air you breathe,

as the money you drop to buy your coffee,

your clothes, your comfort.

I don't need your handouts.

I don't need your good intentions that you put on like a new suit

and feel better about yourself.

I've got no use for your sympathy.

You think that because you live in a building that touches the sky

you're somehow above me?

You think I'm a nobody,

a face you can walk past without a second thought?

But I'm a somebody. I'm real.

And I don't need your approval. I don't need your pity.

I'm the truth in your face

the moment you wake up from your dream and realize you're not so far from me.

When your fortunes collapse, when your warm bed turns cold,

when you can't buy your way out of the shit life throws at you—

I'll still be here,

standing in the wreckage of your perfect little world.

So keep walking, keep pretending you don't see me.

But know this—I'll outlast you.

I've got nothing left to lose. And that's what makes me dangerous.

---

I DON'T NEED YOU TO feel sorry for me, I don't need your soft gaze or your nervous glance. I don't need you to feel like you're doing a good deed when you throw a couple of bucks my way and then hurry off to your "important" life. You think you're doing something? You think that ten dollars buys you a warm, fuzzy feeling, like you're somehow making the world a better place, like you're proving that you have a conscience? Well, you're wrong. Because I don't want your charity. I want your attention, your respect, your real damn acknowledgment. Not your handouts or your fake concern that fades the second you're out of sight.

You walk past me every day, looking away as if I'm some kind of invisible stain on your shiny world. But I'm not invisible. I'm right here, in your face, in your city, standing on the corner while you sip your overpriced coffee, tapping your phone, wearing your perfect clothes, pretending everything is good. I'm not the shadow of your conscience. I'm the reality that you refuse to confront. I'm the person who's just like you except I fell through the cracks you pretend don't exist. And trust me, that's scarier than anything. Because you know deep down you're one bad day, one wrong decision, away from being just like me. But you won't admit that. Not to yourself. Not to anyone. It's too uncomfortable.

But you don't have to look at me, do you? You don't have to feel the weight of my existence pressing on your chest. You can keep going, pretending that as long as you don't make eye contact, I'll just vanish, like I'm not even here, like I'm not breathing the same air as you, walking the same streets, under the same sky. You'll just keep turning your head, shuffling along, pretending that nothing's wrong in your perfect little world.

But here's the thing: I'm not your problem. I'm a mirror. I'm the reflection of a system that's failing, a system that leaves people like me on the street with no options, no dignity. And you can try to ignore me, but you can't outrun the truth. I'm here, and I'm not going anywhere. And one day, you'll look up and realize that this city—your city—has a way of turning people like me into people like you. One wrong step, and the same streets that you walk down every day, that you call your own, will swallow you whole. And when they do, I'll still be here. Watching. Waiting. And I won't turn my head.

# The Memory of a Home

A meditation on loss, nostalgia, and the separation from one's past life before homelessness.

I USED TO LIVE IN A place

where the walls held sound,

and the floors didn't push back

like they were tired of me.

Where there was a kitchen,

and the stove hummed like a heartbeat

in the quiet dark,

the whiff of garlic

burning into the air like life,

not death.

I remember the radiator's cough,

that old thing,

rattling like it was trying

to hold itself together—

so we could stay warm.

But now, I sleep on cracked concrete,

under a streetlight that flickers

like it's giving up,

the light bleeding across my face,

drunk and confused.

The air smells of iron,

wet concrete,

the sour breath of the city,

the wind biting at my bones,

turning them into glass

that breaks every time I move.

I remember the kitchen,

its smallness

as comforting as a lover's arms.

The rug that never really kept the cold out,

but it didn't matter—

it was something to stand on.

I used to breathe the morning in

and think I could do anything.

Now, I stand here,

hollow,

lost in the clutter of strangers' lives,

the people in their suits

walking past me

like I'm a bad smell they can't get rid of.

I try to speak,

but my words turn to ash

before they reach the air.

I used to be someone

who had something to hold onto.

Now, I chase shadows

and they slip right through my fingers.

The old radio I left behind,

the voice of the man on the screen,

the taste of coffee

still lingers in the air of my mind.

But that's all it is now—

just a flicker of warmth

lost in the cold.

I try to hold onto the past,

but it's a house of cards,

blown away with the wind.

I wonder if I ever had a home,

or if it was just an idea

I borrowed from someone else.

Maybe home was never a place.

Maybe it was just a lie

I told myself

to make the cold

more bearable.

———————————

YOU WANT TO KNOW WHAT it's like, huh? To be here, on the street, with nothing but your thoughts and the cold to keep you company? Well, let me tell you, it ain't anything like what they sell you on TV. They want you to believe there's some dignity in this mess, some redemption in every miserable night you spend face down in a pile of trash, shivering, hoping the cops don't roll up and kick your ribs in like they do to everyone else.

But the truth? The truth is you remember the things you had, the life that was once yours. I can still feel the heat from that stove, the crackle of the radiator when the snow piled up outside and I didn't need to wear three layers of rags just to feel my hands. There was a time I sat at the kitchen table and I thought maybe, just maybe, I could make something of myself, could put the pieces back together, like the way I used to fix broken radios with nothing but a screwdriver and a half-baked idea. I had a place. A real place. A home. Can you imagine that? The walls didn't spit back every word I said like they were tired of my voice, like I was too much of a burden. There were rooms that didn't make me feel like I was suffocating in them, that didn't make me hate the feel of my own skin.

Now? Now, I'm a ghost. People walk by and don't see me. Don't even look. I could be dead for all they care. I try to speak but my words fall like rain on stone, unheard. They cross the street, avoid my eyes like I've got some disease they might catch if they get too close. They're better off, right? They've got their shiny lives, their perfect little apartments, their coffee mugs that say shit like "Live, Laugh, Love," like any of that really matters when you can't pay your rent.

But me? I remember. I remember the taste of coffee from a real cup, the sound of a door shutting behind me at night, the feeling of a bed that didn't make my bones ache. I remember a time when I had a choice, when I wasn't invisible. And that's the hardest part, you know? Being erased. You can't even blame the people in suits—no, you can blame the system that sold you out, chewed you up, and spit you out onto the street like you didn't matter. And maybe I don't anymore. But I'm still here, aren't I? Still breathing. Still remembering. That's what they never tell you about being homeless: it's not just the cold that gets to you. It's the memory of the warmth you once had, burning like a damn cigarette you can't put out. And that memory? That's the thing that breaks you the most.

# The Sirens and the Sighs

A piece about the sounds of the city and how they bring both danger and comfort to a homeless person's world.

IN THE MIDDLE OF THE night,

the sirens don't scream—they hum,

like a memory too loud to ignore,

like the only thing left from a life I knew.

They pulse through the city's veins,

a rhythm I can't escape,

its heartbeat frantic,

bloodshot eyes staring back at me

from every storefront window.

I used to think they were for someone else.

Now I know they're for me—

for the ones who vanish

under the weight of the concrete sky.

The sirens are lullabies

sung by ghosts with no names,

each note a promise I can't hear anymore.

Home was a place where the walls were thick with promises—

now broken like glass,

like old windows that never opened

to a world that's no longer mine.

I had a bed once.

Now I sleep on cold pavement

and wake to the same streetlight staring me down,

a beacon for the lost.

The city's breath is my blanket—

full of exhaust fumes and cigarette butts.

It lulls me to sleep,

then drags me back awake

when it's time for me to bleed again.

The sirens sing louder now,

but who's left to listen?

I hear their cries in my sleep,

feel them in the thrum of my bones.

They warn me—

but death's already dancing down the avenue,

and I can't outrun it

even if I try.

The city's always hungry.

It swallows everything in its path,

even the memories of who I was.

But there's comfort in their call,

a warning from the past,

that death and life walk hand-in-hand

through the city streets,

no matter how far we run.

I can't escape the sirens,

but maybe I never wanted to.

———

THE CITY NEVER STOPS making noise. It doesn't give a shit about who's listening or who's dying. The sirens? They're not a warning—they're a part of the soundtrack of this life, like the screech of a subway and the hum of the streetlights. Some people might think they're for the cops, the firemen, or someone else with a little bit of power. But I've learned they're for us—the ones who end up forgotten on the corners, buried under old newspapers and bottles of piss. Those sirens? They belong to us now.

You get used to them after a while, like you get used to the cold biting your bones or the hunger crawling up your throat. It's not that you stop hearing them—it's that you start to feel them in your chest, that rhythm of the city that becomes your own heartbeat. And when you lay down on the sidewalk, curled up like a dog under a blanket made of nothing, you hear the sirens and you don't know if they're there to save you or swallow you whole. Maybe both. Maybe neither.

There's a kind of comfort in it, though. When I hear that wail, I don't think about the houses I used to have, the people who used to care. I think about the rhythm. The way the noise keeps going even after you're gone. The city doesn't stop for anyone—it just keeps swallowing, chewing up everything in its path, and you're part of that now. Your name's gone, your face's gone, but the sound of those sirens will keep echoing down the streets. They're like the last bit of you that survives in the concrete—bleeding, but still alive.

You can't hear the sirens and not feel it, that tightness in your gut. It's the sound of everything you used to know, the life you used to have, falling apart like broken glass. People in their fancy apartments don't hear it the same way. To them, it's just noise, something to complain about, a nuisance, a sign that something's wrong. But to me? It's the sound of a city that doesn't care about who's getting eaten alive by it. It's the sound of survival. And in a way, it's the sound of comfort too.

You hear them? Those sirens? They might be singing for you now. Or for the one who's going to take your place. It doesn't matter. They're still there. They'll always be there, like ghosts of a life you can't remember and a future you can't see. And in the end, that's the only thing that sticks—the sound of everything falling apart, loud and clear, as you fade into the background, swallowed whole by the city.

# Letters to No One

The idea of writing letters or journals that no one ever reads, a form of
self-expression that's never acknowledged.

1.

I WRITE TO NO ONE,

words that will fall through the cracks,

lost in the smoke of another bad memory.

They're not for you,

they're for me—

but I still expect you to read them,

I need you to read them,

or else why the hell do I bother?

I write about the cold,

the way it gnaws at my bones,

but that's just the surface.

It's deeper than the cold—

it's this city,

this endless scream of steel and concrete

that pulls me in,

chews me up,

spits me out

to wander this night

where nothing matters,

except the quiet breath I steal

while the world keeps on tearing itself apart.

I write about the stars I can't see anymore,

the ones that slipped behind the smog,

and the dreams I buried

so deep they smell like rot.

I used to care about the stars.

I used to believe in something.

Not anymore.

Now, I write because

the words are mine,

even if no one gives a damn.

The sirens keep coming.

They scream louder now,

like they're mocking me,

the city's heart beating faster,

like it knows we're all out of time.

## HOMELESS IN NEW YORK

I've seen the rats scurrying in the alleys,

I've heard them gnaw at the truth,

I've felt their teeth sink into my skin—

but I'm still here.

Still writing letters to no one.

I scribble down a memory,

maybe two,

but they don't last,

just slip like oil through my fingers.

What's the use?

Who's gonna care about my words?

They're all drowning in their own noise,

in their own shiny plastic lives,

pretending they're better than me

while I sit here and watch them

with their hands full of nothing.

The letters,

the journals,

the scribbles on napkins

and scraps of paper,

they're nothing more

than the empty bottles

that roll underfoot—

empty, useless,

but still there.

Still clinking around,

screaming for attention

that no one gives.

I write because I've got nothing else,

because silence eats at the soul.

And maybe, just maybe,

these words,

this mess,

this ugly truth,

will slip through the cracks

and find you somehow,

find someone who hears.

But until then,

I'll keep writing to no one.

To no one at all.

———————————

2.

———————————

I SIT HERE, WATCHING the world pass by,

a thousand stories whizzing past me like ghosts—

they don't see me. They never see me.

They're too busy chasing the same damn thing I was chasing once.

But here I am, with nothing but a pen

and a scrap of paper,

writing letters to no one,

because that's what I've got left—

a few words scribbled down in the dark,

like a fool hoping someone,

somewhere,

might give a shit.

It's funny, isn't it?

How you can be surrounded by thousands of people

and still feel invisible?

Like you're just some kind of shadow,

stumbling through the cracks of the city,

waiting for something to crack open,

waiting for someone to notice,

but they won't.

They can't.

They've got their own crap to deal with,

their own delusions to feed.

And I get it.

Who wants to look at the broken pieces?

Who wants to smell the rot when their own house

is built of glass?

But me?

I write.

I write because the silence is worse.

The silence is a hundred times louder than the screams.

I've got all these words in me,

but no one's listening.

The city's too damn loud—

sirens, cars, people pretending they don't care.

And yet, I keep scribbling these words down,

like they mean something,

like they'll make a difference.

But who's gonna read 'em?

Who's gonna care?

I'm just another guy,

just another shadow in a city full of shadows,

another lost soul with nothing to offer

but a few ugly truths.

These letters? They're all I have left.

They're the last scraps of me

that haven't been swallowed whole by the city,

the last thing that reminds me

I'm still here.

I'm still breathing.

And maybe that's enough.

Maybe I don't need anyone else to hear it.

Maybe it's enough that I can still write

to no one,

and somehow,

feel a little less invisible.

It's a lie, of course.

A damn lie.

But it's the only one that doesn't make me feel

like I'm already dead.

---

I DON'T EXPECT ANYONE to read this. Hell, I don't expect anyone to even care that I wrote it. But I'll tell you anyway, just because it's all I've got. I used to have a life—some kind of life. I had a bed, a roof, a paycheck that didn't stretch enough to make me feel like a real person, but it was something. It was more than this. This dirt. This concrete. This garbage. I used to be someone who mattered—at least, that's what I thought. Now, I'm invisible. And if I'm being honest, it's like that's the only thing that's real anymore. The people with their shiny faces, their leather shoes, their perfect lives—they can walk right past me. It's like I'm nothing. Like I don't even exist.

The sirens are there. Screaming and wailing In the distance like some kind of fucking clockwork. The city's heartbeat, and I'm just caught in the wake of it. Every night, I hear the same noise. The same damn urgency. And I wonder, who's it for? It's like it's not even for me. Not that I expect it to be. I'm just another body on the sidewalk, just another piece of trash for the rats to nibble on, or maybe for the cops to kick while they're rounding up the junkies. I hear the sirens, I feel the tremors in the street, and I think to myself: 'What's the difference between them and me?' I'm just another lost soul that no one will save, another forgotten man with nothing but these scraps of paper to tell my story. No one's going to listen. I can write these letters till my hand falls off, but they won't be read. They're just my thoughts bleeding into the pages—thoughts that will die here, alone, in the dirt.

But what else is there? What else can I do but write my thoughts down like a madman? Maybe it's not about being read, after all. Maybe it's just about writing so that I don't forget I'm still alive. 'Still alive.' That's the joke, isn't it? Everyone else is running around pretending they've got something to live for. A family. A job. A dream. And here I am, scribbling away, writing to no one, because it's the only thing left that makes me feel like I haven't been completely erased.

They don't see me. They don't hear me. But at least I can still write. Even if no one reads it. Even if I never matter to anyone but myself. At least I can still bleed onto these pages.

# The Rain Never Stops in the City

A reflection on how nature, like the rain, seems to ignore the homeless, and how they endure it.

IT RAINS IN THIS CITY

like it's got a goddamn point to prove

and we're all left under it

drowning in the slick of our skin,

stuck in the gaps between the concrete

where no one gives a damn

if your shoes fill up

or your fingers go numb.

it comes down,

the rain—hard as fists,

hammering,

but you keep moving through it

as if you're meant to.

you curl up beneath cardboard,

watch the drip-drip of the world

falling on your face,

and wonder if it's the sky or your soul

that's crying.

letters are all I have left—

and I write them like no one will ever see them.

they're scratched on paper,

penned with dry hands

that know better than to ask for pity,

that know better than to beg

for a place to rest.

these letters are to no one.

they'll never be read.

I write because there's nothing else.

I write because the rain keeps coming,

and it's all I've got

to drown out the noise

of a city that keeps moving

past my wet, aching body,

past the ghosts of my old life

that were once so damn important.

there's no warmth in the letters

just wet ink and broken thoughts,

each word slipping like water

down the page.

there's no end to this rain,

and there's no end to the hunger,

either.

but I keep writing.

I write because sometimes,

in the cold black night,

I wonder if maybe

the rain will stop

if I ask it enough times.

maybe I'll be seen

by someone who's not too busy

to notice a body,

to notice a soul

that keeps aching for a way out.

but the rain doesn't stop.

it never does.

it only gets louder.

and in the end,

I guess that's all I've ever been—

a letter to no one.

another body lost in the flood,

another soul

left to drown

in the dark.

———————

THE RAIN NEVER STOPS in this city. It's like some sick joke, a damn punishment no one talks about. People walking by, heads tucked into their collars, eyes trained straight ahead—like they're too good to notice the bodies lying in the puddles, the feet that never quite get warm, the hands too worn out to pray anymore. It's all just noise, the splash of water on the sidewalk, the hum of the streets, the rush of people who don't see you anymore. But the rain? The rain's the only thing that gives a damn. Not because it cares, but because it doesn't.

You'd think it would stop, eventually. Some kind of mercy. But that's not how it works in this city. The rain falls all night, all day, without a single fuck to give. And what do you do with it? You don't do anything. You just let it soak through you, let it find the cracks in your skin and slip in. You're not worth the umbrella. You're not worth the coat, the jacket, the comfort of a dry corner. That's for the people walking by, the ones who don't see you, the ones who couldn't care less. They won't ever know what it feels like when the water's running down your bones, eating at your muscles, pulling every inch of warmth from your skin. They don't know what it's like to have your soul bleeding out from under your feet while you keep walking, knowing you've got nowhere to go. The rain doesn't stop. It just keeps coming, like time, like life, like all those years that slipped away without anyone noticing.

And still, you write. You write because that's all that's left. The paper doesn't care, the ink doesn't care. It's just you and the rain, scratching your words onto something that'll never be read, something that'll never matter. It's like throwing a stone in the ocean, watching it sink, knowing it'll never be seen again. But you do it anyway. Because maybe, just maybe, there's someone out there who'll understand. Someone who'll know what it's like to live in the shadow of something bigger, colder, darker. Someone who'll feel your words in their gut, even if they never read them. Even if they never stop.

But the rain? It doesn't stop. It never does. And neither do you.

# Wanderers Under the Brooklyn Bridge

The sense of community formed by those who find shelter under the iconic structure.

UNDER THE ARCHES, A world without clocks,

no lines drawn, just a map of cold shadows—

those who wander and those who have been left

to breathe the city's dust and rain,

a downpour that never stops,

like the memory of someone who has walked away

and never returned.

The bridge looms,

a silent giant,

cracking beneath the weight of its own refusal.

It doesn't care,

doesn't ask for your name or your soul,

just shelters you

from the things that want to break you—

the rain, the heat, the noise

that pushes like a fist against your skull.

The others are here, too.

They sleep between the columns,

a ragged congregation

whose prayers are unheard.

Some say it's the hunger,

but hunger doesn't care for names either.

It doesn't stop when you beg,

just keeps eating you alive

until there's nothing left to take.

They speak in whispers,

but it's a language the city never learns,

the sound of broken hope,

of dreams crumbling like brick dust.

Still, there's something here—

a kind of belonging,

under this great, indifferent stone,

as if we've created our own gravity

in the face of the world's indifference.

The rain doesn't care—

it's not here to cleanse.

It's here to remind you

how small you are

against a sky that doesn't stop,

against a world that never notices

you're still alive,

waiting for the day it all ends.

But there is something,

even in this,

a defiance that whispers

between the rivets and the cracks.

We survive,

though no one asks us to,

and the bridge listens,

but never speaks—

it holds us

in the silence of its shadow,

and we keep on,

waiting for something to change,

or for nothing to change at all.

---

THE CITY DOESN'T CARE if I'm here. The streets don't pause for me, they don't even flinch. I'm just another piece of debris, swept to the side when the wind picks up. You learn quickly that no one gives a damn about you until you're dead. People walk by, and it's like I'm invisible, a blur at the corner of their eye. They don't see me because they can't afford to. They don't want to see what's real when the gloss of their lives is so shiny and clean. I don't fit into that. And the thing is, I don't care anymore. I don't need to fit.

Under the Brooklyn Bridge, I found the kind of freedom you don't get in the city's shiny apartments. There's no rent, no bullshit promises, no landlords sucking the life out of you. Here, the only thing that matters is survival. There's a peace in that. It's brutal, raw peace, like a knife against your ribs, but it's peace. The rain comes down like it's trying to drown you, but you don't mind it. It's honest, unlike the people who've long forgotten what it's like to struggle. The rain doesn't lie—it doesn't care who you are. It'll hit you just as hard as it hits anyone else. And that's the thing, you see—out here, it's just you against the world. There's no pretending. No filters. No masks. Just survival, and sometimes, survival feels like an act of rebellion in this city of lies.

Under the bridge, there are others, like me, lost but found in a way. We share the space, the shadows, the silence. Sometimes there's a kind of unspoken bond between us, a solidarity that doesn't need words. We know what it's like to be overlooked, to be discarded. We've lived it. We've been chewed up by this world, spit out, and we keep moving, even when it feels like we can't anymore. It's not about hope anymore. It's about enduring. Just enduring the fucking rain, the cold, the hunger. It's enough.

They think we're weak, or lost, or maybe we're just a reminder of everything they're afraid to become. But they don't understand. They can't. Because we don't need to be saved. We've already saved ourselves by not giving in. By staying under this bridge, by surviving it all without the world ever knowing.

# The Color of Asphalt

*The grayness of life on the streets, where even the colors are muted and unimportant.*

THE CITY SPITS GRAY like it was born for it,

pavement swallowing the colors of the living.

Here, the sky is just a promise we've forgotten,

the buildings make sure you know it's too late.

Under the bridge, where the rats and the angels

dance in shadow, I've made my bed—

a mattress of cardboard,

a blanket of wet trash bags.

I sleep and I wait,

my bones aching

but my heart still raw with the refusal to disappear.

The rain doesn't stop.

It falls like a judgement,

like the city is washing its hands of us.

You'd think it would end,

but it doesn't.

# HOMELESS IN NEW YORK

It's a shiver that cuts through the bones,

but you get used to it,

just like the hunger.

I used to think there was color in the world—

red like the blood I lost

and the love I squandered,

blue like the skies I never see,

but now I'm just another ghost

slipping through this gray hell

that calls itself a city.

You've got your shiny windows,

your people who don't know the meaning of real hunger,

your men in suits pretending to matter,

while the streets get covered in piss and ash,

and the faces you pass

are no more than shadows

you refuse to look at.

And me, I'm nothing but the smell

of stale breath and wet clothes—

I'm a rumor,

an unwanted question,

a whisper that never gets answered.

I could crawl into your world,

sit down at your bar,

but you wouldn't let me in.

You'd call the cops.

You'd call me a beggar.

You'd make sure I'm not seen.

But I'm still here.

You might not look, but I'm here.

It's the gray that takes you down—

the constant hum of nothingness

that makes you forget what you were

before the streets claimed you.

Before the city chewed you up

and spit you out like another faded coat

discarded on the sidewalk.

So you drink in the rain,

the bitter taste of survival

mixing with the city's indifference.

And tomorrow, it'll rain again.

And the gray will press in harder,

but you'll stand,

because that's all we can do now—

stand against the weight

of the world

that doesn't even see us.

———————

YOU WANT ME TO EXPLAIN it, huh? This poem? Like it's a puzzle or something. Nah, man, this is just the truth—raw and ugly. The thing you don't want to hear, the thing that's too close to the bone. You don't want to look too long at it. You'd rather turn your head, pretend it's not there, right? But the truth is, it's everywhere. It's all around you, crawling on the sidewalk, eating from garbage cans, living in doorways. You think we're invisible? We aren't. We're just waiting for the rain to stop so we can take another breath.

See, this city—it don't give a damn about you. Doesn't matter if you were born in it or if you just stumbled in from nowhere. It's a machine. A cold one. And it grinds down anything that gets too close to it. You want a color? You think this city is full of life and color? Ha! What color is the street? What color is your suit, your shiny shoes, the ones you think make you better than me? Gray. That's what it is. Just a blanket of gray. The buildings. The pavement. The sky—if you even see it. The only color here is the red of blood when someone gets hit. Or the bruises under your eyes when the nights drag on too long. It's the gray that takes away everything that used to matter. It makes you forget who you were. Makes you stop remembering your name, your dreams, your past.

You think it's just about the rain? It's not. Sure, the rain comes down and makes everything stick to you, the weight of the world gets heavier with every drop, but that's not the problem. The problem is the grayness, the indifference, the way the city just keeps spinning without a thought for who falls off. You can stand there in your fancy coat, huddled under your umbrella, looking down your nose at the rest of us. You think you've made it, right? You think you've beaten the game. But let me tell you something—you haven't. Not really. Because the city has this way of making you forget what it is to live, to feel. You just become a shadow in the rain. And I've been a shadow so long, I don't even know what light looks like anymore.

So yeah, I'm here. In the gray. In the rain. I'm here and I'll still be here, even when you close your eyes and pretend I'm not.

# Epilogue: A Letter to the Lucky Ones

———

Hey, you over there, in the warm, dry apartment with the soft sheets and the refrigerator full of food. You with the steady job and the predictable life. The ones who only see us as the stain on the city's perfect face. The ones who walk by without a second thought, avoiding our eyes like we might infect you with something contagious. You, who will never know what it feels like to wake up every morning not knowing if you'll have a place to sleep that night. Yeah, you. You who think you're untouchable, safe behind that door, locked away from the mess of the world out here.

I'm gonna tell you something you'll never understand, something you'd rather not know. Because if you did, it might change how you see everything, and I know you don't want that. It's easier to keep the world in its neat little boxes, right? So, you can keep telling yourself the lie that we're nothing more than some mistake of nature. Some aberration, a broken piece of the machine you're too busy polishing to notice.

We live out here, on the sidewalks and under bridges, in alleys and forgotten corners. But that's not what you think. You think we're all the same—drunk, crazy, lazy, violent, criminal. You see us and you cross the street. You see us and you flinch. You look down at your shiny shoes and pretend we don't exist. But you don't know anything about us, and if you did, you'd wish you could un-know it.

We were once like you, once, before the world came crashing down on us. Maybe we were a little too honest, too proud, too raw. Or maybe we just got caught in the wrong moment, the wrong break. Life's a game of roulette, and sometimes, the wheel doesn't stop where you expect it. Sometimes, you don't get to choose.

So don't tell me we're here because we made bad choices. Don't tell me it's our fault. Don't you dare sit there, smug and cozy in your comfortable chair, talking about "personal responsibility." Like you've never been a few bad decisions away from this. Like you've never had the rug pulled out from under you. You think you're safe in your little bubble, but let me tell you something: you're one layoff, one health crisis, one car accident away from being right here, on the same pavement, eating out of the same trash cans, begging for spare change, just like the rest of us.

You see, there's no dignity here. No privacy. No luxury. Just cold concrete and the smell of piss in the alleyways, and the echo of your own footsteps as you walk by. You walk past us like we're invisible, like we're not human anymore. But we are. We bleed. We breathe. We dream.

You don't see it, but we've got stories, stories that would make you squirm, stories that would make you rethink your life. We've got memories, we've got pasts, and some of us still have hope buried deep down inside. It's buried, but it's there. Maybe just a flicker, a shadow of something that used to be a fire. You wouldn't know that because you look at us like we're already dead, like we've given up, like we're just waiting to fade into the background. But we haven't. We're still here. And we'll be here, no matter how much you try to ignore us.

We've watched you, too. We've seen the way you move through your lives, heads down, running to your next thing, barely glancing at the people around you. We see you rush past the homeless shelter, the line for food, the men and women begging for change. You don't even hear their voices anymore. You don't even hear the desperation in their pleas. Because if you did, it might make you feel something, and you've got no time for that. You've got bills to pay, and a career to build, and a house to keep up.

You think your problems are the real ones. You think your anxiety, your stress, your job drama, your relationship issues, your damn car payments—those are the things that matter. You think the homeless guy on the corner doesn't have it worse than you, but let me tell you, you have no idea. You have no idea what it's like to lie awake at night with the rain pouring down, trying to figure out where you'll sleep next, whether it'll be under that bridge with the rats and the piss or in the back of a restaurant parking lot where the smell of grease lingers like a curse.

You think you've got problems? Try this on for size: waking up in the morning with the knowledge that no matter what, your day's gonna suck. Because there's nowhere to go. No job, no house, no purpose. Just you and the cold, and maybe a bottle of cheap whiskey or some dirty needle to take the edge off. You want to talk about stress? You've never known stress until you've been in our shoes, until you've had to fight for every breath, every scrap, every damn bit of dignity you can salvage from this hellhole.

And when we do talk to you, when we do ask for help, you look away, don't you? You avoid our eyes, like we're contagious, like we're some kind of threat. You think you can't help, that you're too busy, too caught up in your perfect little world to stop for just a second and see us as human beings. But it's easier that way, isn't it? Easier to ignore us than to face the uncomfortable truth. Easier to write us off as "junkies" or "bums" than to admit that you could be one of us. Because deep down, you know that all it takes is one misstep, one cruel twist of fate, and there you are, cold and hungry and forgotten.

We're not invisible. Not really. We see you. We see the way you turn your back on us, the way you pretend we don't exist. But we're here. We've always been here. We're not going anywhere.

So the next time you pass us by, don't look away. Don't ignore us like we're ghosts. Remember this: we are the truth you can't hide from. We are the reality that you pretend doesn't exist. And whether you like it or not, we're part of your world. You've just forgotten that.

# About Alex Telman

ALEX TELMAN IS A PROLIFIC poet whose works encompass sonnets, sestinas, and modern poetic forms. His poetry captures the essence of life in both urban and rural settings, delving into the psychological and philosophical depths of the human experience. Recognized for their profound insight, his poems weave realism with emotional richness, offering readers a deeper understanding of life's complexities.

# Don't miss out!

Visit the website below and you can sign up to receive emails whenever Alex Telman publishes a new book. There's no charge and no obligation.

https://books2read.com/r/B-A-YBSCC-DBJIF

**BOOKS2READ**

Connecting independent readers to independent writers.

www.ingramcontent.com/pod-product-compliance
Lightning Source LLC
Chambersburg PA
CBHW071415150726
48000CB00001B/341